# The Victors of Arkanya

Anthony E. Gaiani Jr

NEWMAN SPRINGS PUBLISHING
320 Broad Street
Red Bank, NJ 07701

First originally published by Newman Springs Publishing 2022

ISBN 978-1-68498-326-1 (Paperback)
ISBN 978-1-68498-327-8 (Digital)

Printed in the United States of America

For my family and friends, for without their unyielding
love and support, this book would not exist.

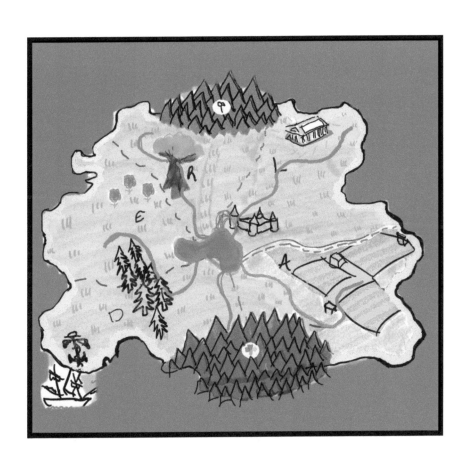

# Prologue

Hey there, yes you! Okay, so you know what you just grabbed off the—what do you call them—shelves? No, of course not. Nobody does. That's why so many people have so many questions. Do you ever find that people in life would have fewer questions if they (for once) sought the answers they claim to seek? You grabbed something special. This book is more than just a story. In it are the lives of so many people, some of whom are sadly no longer with us. Why you ask? It's… You know what, I don't think you're ready. I won't tell you why unless you make a deal with me. What you're asking is not a simple close-ended question; where the answer lies is going to require perseverance, bravery, strength, and confidence and, above all, love. It's going to be grand in scale and size but also terrifying and hard to witness; it'll be as beautiful as your mother's smile in the morning sun but as cold as a war in winter. I can hear you laughing at this. If you're not serious about your own question, we don't have to go anywhere. You can put this back on the shelf and go your merry way. But if you think happiness is important, you owe it to yourself to take an adventure with me. Happiness is very important to life. It's powerful because of what it yields: peace. Peace is something people, for a millennium, have fought wars to keep (ironic, right?); it's also something that people everywhere, every day, wish they had more of. That's the thing about peace. Life can throw us so many challenges and trials that we may sometimes feel like we have an unfair balance, but that is what makes peace so special: its elite quantity, its rarity, and its precious, fragile, harmonious existence. To ever not have happiness is not only a miserable state, but it can also be dangerous. In the absence of happiness, dark can succeed. *Dark* here means anger or depression, or worse, vengeance. Go without happiness for too long and sometimes we become our own villain and cause harm to ourselves. Can you imagine that? Someone being so unhappy that they'd rather die than continue the life they have—their unique blessing of a life. Still think happiness is nice but unimportant? Okay then, take a seat. This is for you.

Okay, so the deal is this: I'll answer your question of how those people died and what happened if and only if you answer some things for me. Sounds fair? These are big questions too, so go ahead and grab your favorite drink, take a seat, and hear me out. Ready? Okay, let's begin. First question: What is/was the happiest time in your life? It can be anything, but I am not talking about a random object someone you care about gifted you. I'm talking about the kind of happiness that stands the test of time and years later, still has the ability to make you smile. Close your eyes and think for a moment; sift through all your happy thoughts and find the strongest one you can. You got it, your moment? Okay, great. Hold on to that. You're smiling, aren't you? Isn't it funny how something as insignificant as happiness can bring a smile to your face, even though I guarantee you that memory you have in your mind's eye right now is old? That is the point, that life can sometimes be stressful, scary, or uncertain, but happiness, even after the event ends, lingers and transcends time. Pretty powerful, isn't it? Get ready, I'll ask you your final question now.

Second question: Can you think of a time in your life when you had absolutely no happiness, no hope, and all you had was isolation or despair? Dramatic, I know, but answer it, please. Again, I'm not talking about a test you failed; I'm talking about the kind of despair from loss, from betrayal, or from feeling like you don't matter. Do you have your moment? Hey, it's okay if you're crying, or if you feel tense right now. That's what darkness does. *But* darkness (unhappiness) is every bit as much a part of who we are as happiness is. It is not our past that defines our character but rather how we handle strife or mistakes and pain. Do we learn from any of those missteps to prevent the bad event from happening to us again, or do we wallow in pity and blind ourselves to its second act? I am here to tell you a novel idea you're probably not going to like: Pain is actually a good thing; it can be a teacher, if you acknowledge the pain and address the core, and it helps shed light on how to avoid feeling it again. Growth, maturity, thicker skin, and so forth are all lessons we can glean from addressing pain. Do you see why you're here now? You are helping me a lot, and we don't even know each other. You know, it's funny you remind me of my brother. Ah, anyway, I'll give you the same blessing my mother gave me the day she died: "Be kind, have strength, and love always,."

Speaking of pain, I miss my mom. She died…a long time ago, Twenty-nine years ago, in fact. Now that you understand the importance of happiness, it's time I take you to where our adventure begins, to where your answers lie: my home, Arkanya. Here, take this rune, smash it on your chest, and grab my arm. Do not let go of me! I'll see you on the other side.

# 1

# Pax Arkanya

Once upon a time, in the farthest reaches of the known universe stands the deeply magical kingdom called Arkanya. Now Arkanya is such an enormous planet that it is divided into regions or Palacorns. In the northeast Palacorn of Arkanya lies the quiet but ever so important region of Leonulia. Named for one of the stars in the night sky, this region is famed for its religious festivals, feasts, and peaceful culture. The inhabitants content themselves with family and friends and generally make their living by preaching, farming, or teaching. The arts and trades so strongly present here are passed on passionately from parent to child to grandchild, and so forth. The transference of love intertwines with the skill sets and tools required, yielding not just beautiful buildings, homes, and schools but also strong creations that have remained unfazed from every storm and weather calamity thus far.

Far out in the northeast of Arkanya lies one of the most important locations on the entire map, for inside this temple lies all the world's known prophecies. Stacked neatly in line like a row of books, the prophecies shine like a mosaic rainbow. An ancient wizard donning a shimmering white-and-brown cloak pores over rows upon rows of glowing, magical orbs. Each orb is a new shade of light and color.

Some believe this is the oldest building in Arkanya. Quite possibly, it is the first ever constructed. Nevertheless, the craftsmanship of this one building dictates the architectural style of the country. To the outside, it will appear as a hybrid of Gothic and art deco. Stained glass, gold, and rich woods are used every bit as much as marble, polished to such a fine shine that it deceives all who entered, thinking the walls are wet. The marble walls and ceilings are of white, green, and red color while the floors are made of lapis lazuli, a foreign material brought to Arkanya by a mysterious traveler long ago.

The hooded wizard mulls over a glowing orb, attempting to read its secrets when a mother and son walk toward the exit. Though the temple is home to the prophecies, it is also a library. The wizard's name is Yidnar. He has a wife, Liefadra, whom he met when he was just a small lad, but more on that later. Yidnar is a tall, thin, and tanned gentleman with a pointy, long beard, a pointy, thin nose, and pointy, long fingers. He is like a hodgepodge of personality traits— warm yet serious, stern and sometimes stubborn yet open-minded, loyal but also nonconforming. He has a strong moral compass, which time and time again proved unshakable. He is indeed the oldest man in the world. By appearances, you'll think he is just completing time at the university. Inwardly, however, Yidnar is, in point of fact, present at the birth of this great nation thousands of years prior. The people of Arkanya, though, do not believe that last bit. They understand him to be older than he looks, but do not think that means to say he was there when all was created.

"Do you think he was alive when Arkanya was made?" a child asks. He has a curled mass of bright-red hair and a face peppered with tiny freckles. His wide, blue eyes gaze in wonder and intrigue at the mysterious Yidnar.

"Of course not, sweetie. Don't say such things," his mother says in rebuttal while also laughing. The mother wears an odd collection of colors, as if she is competing with the mosaic of the organized, glowing, colored prophecies. Her coat is patched a thousand times over, and each time with a different color and material. Her hair is bright red and frizzy, and her face is filled with a desire to sleep. She loves her son, but he is also exhausting.

Mage Yidnar then grins at the family as they walk toward the exit of the temple and he shares eye contact with the child. As their eyes meet, Yidnar winks as if to say, "Why yes, I was there when Arkanya was born!" But who could say? And they leave.

Mage Yidnar tends to his specialty: decoding and translating encrypted prophecies to determine if they are mere fortunes or if they shall actually come to pass. His hands pierce through the glowing, fragile orbs of prophetic magic with such ease; it is as if the orbs are not solid. His eyes begin to glow bright orange as his magic narrows in on the message of the prophecy. Yidnar uses another hand to translate the inscription from an ancient tongue no longer used in Arkanya. Finally, the entire script is decoded, and with both hands he gestures as if opening a large scroll before him. With a swirl of wind and a flash of orange light from his magic, the prophecy floats before him in brightly illuminated magical letters. Sadly revealing that this prophecy is not to come to pass. Yidnar lets out a sigh of frustration and wipes his brow of sweat.

In Arkanya, it is important to note that magic is not unfamiliar. In fact, one in every seven citizens (on average) has magic. Magic here though is somewhat different. For a genadenz (those without magic), the only actions they can take regarding magic are the following:

1.  Drink potions
2.  Attempt to use runes

The word *attempt* here is key. While a rune may have been crafted by a mage with the purpose of healing minor wounds, shall a genadenz individual use said rune, there is no telling what can actually occur. Maybe it will not only heal the wounds but also cure any other ailments? Or maybe it will amputate whichever body part the rune is used on! Magic for those without the magika blood cell is both highly unpredictable and extremely dangerous and potentially lethal. As a result, it makes magic extremely risky for them. A genadenz can certainly pick up a magic staff and attempt to cast a spell; however, nothing will happen other than their own embarrassment. The staff will function no different than a regular stick from a dead tree. For it is absolutely true to say that a real magical staff bound to a fellow magakos, is very much alive and connects with its master through the magika blood cell. The casting of a spell with wands or staves in Arkanya is not required (meaning spells can be cast without staves or wands) but is highly respected and adored. It is the symbol of a wizard's or witch's solemn love of Arkanya, their oath to help and protect others. It is for this reason that typically when a genadenz family requests a mentor for a family member, they will ask for a magakos individual.

I mentioned earlier that in order to use magic correctly, one needs the magika blood cell. There are two criteria that must be met in order for magic to be present in an Arkanyan person:

1. The person's biological mother and father must have fallen in true love before and during conception of a child.
2. The biological parents while in true love with each other must also believe in an afterlife.

Then and only then can a person have magic, and the magika blood cell is given to the child, not the parents. This means several important things. First, while it is possible and a good idea for someone who has the magika blood cell to train their arkane skills and learn more, it is *not* possible to train a genadenz to use magic and do anything other than drink potions and use runes (because again, the outcomes of both are unpredictable and arguably not worth the gamble).

Second, for the magakos (those with the magika blood cell), the use and practice of magic can be exhausting over time. Casting spells requires physical and arkane energy, so using magic for prolonged periods of time becomes tiring. If one is fighting opponents, casting defensive and offensive spells left and right, after a few minutes, the person will likely be panting and sweating. Too much time casting spells, and you'll need to recharge. How do you recharge magic? Why, that depends entirely upon what your innate arkane blessing is. Each magakos person has one unique ability, the arkane blessing, which determines how their magic energy replenishes after exhaustion. If for example a magakos girl has the arkane blessing of reading minds, to recharge her magic she will need to meditate and relax; a magakos with the arkane blessing to be invisible will need to be in as crowded an area as possible; likewise, a magakos man whose arkane ability is to control one of the elements, his method of recharging will include the naturally occurring source of that element. While every magakos Arkanyan has a unique ability, all magakos have telekinesis, telepathic communication, high athletic abilities (perfect balance, fast running speeds, etc.), and a sixth sense: detection of like magic. This means that someone who has a particular focus on a type of magic (combat, stealth, regeneration, elemental, etc.) can sense the presence of another magakos person who has the same magical focus. Magical focus simply is personal preference, and it is also possible to heavily train in all brands of magic.

In Arkanya, magic is not unfamiliar, but it is fairly rare. Again, only one in every seven, on average, have magic and as such, the government of the world has had to adapt over time. The laws in place are not specific enough to reprimand or commend those with magic. Centuries ago, it became paramount to have a separate set of laws that only applied to the magakos. All regular laws apply to everyone, but in addition to statutory law (the aforementioned regular laws), there is also arkane law comprised of three components:

1. No person, animal, foreigner, or any other being (living, dead, undead, cursed, or otherwise animated) shall ever, under any circumstances, use magic to banish another to a different land.
2. No person, animal, foreigner, or any other being (living, dead, undead, cursed, or otherwise animated) shall ever, under any circumstances, use magic to kill, harm, disable, or in any other way, temporary or permanent, negatively affect another.
3. Laws 1 and/or 2 *can* be broken if and only if it is to protect the High Archon or High Reina, his/her Palacorn Ministers, anyone else within Arkanya and within eyesight of her borders.

These laws are brought upon by the current High Archon, Separtino, who, a thousand years ago, defeated the only villains Arkanya has ever faced. In a glorious battle between monster and Arkanyan soldier, the High Archon casted a spell that took away magic from all living things at the time, including himself and supposedly, the King of Torment, the Lord of Malice, Kalypto.

Just as Mage Yidnar has taken a break out of annoyance with not discovering a Propheta Fior (a prophecy which will come to pass), there blows the sound of trumpets as the High Archon's guard marches down the streets of Leonulia to alert the citizens of their ruler's coming announcements.

# 2

# The Descent

The Palace of the Falls buzzes with activity, making preparations for the Rex's coming World Address; this is what it's called when the reigning Rex or Rexa speaks directly to their subjects on the Balcony of Defeat. The Palace of the Falls is so named because immediately at its base lies a raging river that drops off almost directly at the edge of the Palace Grounds, descending nearly 1,001 feet to the enchanted lake below. The waters in Lake Souviens are a magical compound. Glowing bright cobalt blue and magenta, Lake Souviens's glow can be seen on the faces of nearby onlookers even during the day. There are many genadenz who stir up rumors of what magical properties the lake might have, but the one true property is one of memory and love. When the two moons are both full and bright, should any magakos Arkanyan enter the lake by foot and allow the water to cover their knees, they will have the opportunity to see the spirit of a lost loved one. The palace, by the way, is quite a sight to be seen.

The palace is made entirely out of the glimmering marble quarried from the Schrie Mountains in the north. The marble pours out from the base of the castle walls, forming a beautiful "spill" on the ground as the palace's foundation. Within the asymmetrical spill patterns, stairs to the ground-level are carved, gilded, and draped in red velvet. The ornate flooring remains constant in design until entering the interior of the ground floor of the palace, at which point the velvet-covered gilded marble is then replaced with lapis lazuli. A brilliant bright-blue foreign stonelike sapphire sparkles for as far as two thousand acres. Each floor is adorned with crown molding, cantilevered interior balconies, enchanted, levitating, magical crystal chandeliers, enchanted flowers from the Heatherlyn forest, and ceilings hand-painted by artisans from the faithful region of Leonulia. Each domed ceiling depicts a region of Arkanya: the farmlands in the southeast of Acamaro, the enchanted flower meadows in the northeast of Earth, the mountains of Regulusio, the swift green countryside of Leonulia, and the shores and oceanfront of Denebia in the southwest. There is no denying that this is the center of government and the home for the ruler of Arkanya.

Each floor is eighty feet high and devoted to the home office for each of the Rex's second-in-command, his prime scepters. There is one prime scepter for each Palacorn. This assists them in handling affairs of state, commerce, governance, revenue, and the like. On the exterior, at each point of the pentagonal-shaped palace is a tower that soars fifty feet higher than the overall structure, which is already four hundred feet tall. There are claw marks, teeth marks, and gnarled twisted metal plates on the roof of the palace that can still be seen on a clear day. This damage is now sacred, as it is remnants of the Great War between the Rex of Arkanya, Separtino, and the Lord of Malice, Kalypto, a thousand years ago. The damage, however, is not brought by either person, but rather the most revered, most sacred of all Arkanya's beasts, the creators of the magic in this land, the mighty and good Drakulogons. Since the defeat of Kalypto a thousand years ago today, the Drakulogons have not been seen.

All throughout the land, the High Archon's guards stand at attention in formation along all banks of the Eirini River. The soldiers march smartly in their ceremonial garb catch the attention of Arkanyans, young and old alike. There has not been an event half as glittering and peppered with high-ranking dignitary appearances in an age.

"Attention, people of Arkanya, your ruler and reigning Rex, the High Archon Separtino!" announces the captain of the Rex's guard.

"My fellow Arkanyans, your home, our home, has faced something more persistent and longer lasting than any of her former foes in history. Peace! We, my fellow Arkanyans, should rejoice! We have had peace in our world for the past one thousand years! Be proud of your lands! Be thankful to our protective forces and rejoice my friends. Here's to another one thousand years of peace!" As the Rex of Arkanya proclaims the day to be Victory in Arkanya Day, the nation ignites into a thunderous roar of cheers, applause, and excitement. Then the Rex raises one hand to bring silence.

"Loyal subjects, we have more reason to celebrate. The two most precious, most cherished states of being in our culture are those of peace and love. So it is my pleasure to introduce you to your new Rexa, Descendia of Denebia!" As the Rex speaks, he stands shimmering in his gilded robes and gem-studded crown. Oddly though, an ominous cloud settles in and casts a peculiar dark shadow over his crown, causing it to lay an extraordinarily dim atop his head, hidden therefore almost entirely. He steps to the side, allowing his one true love, Descendia, to step forward to the edge of the white marble balcony.

As Descendia approaches the marbled rail on the balcony, the country erupts yet again in deafening applause and cheer for her radiant beauty. Her dark skin complements her light-red hair; she wears an amethyst-encrusted gown with draping ruby-studded sleeves. The waist is at an angle and not symmetrical, nor is her neckline open and warm; rather, it is tightly woven, and the material switches from the beautiful purple stone to a subdued black silk with seams that looks like a great spider has woven the bodice, inspired by his own web. She shares a loving glance at her fiancé, the Rex of Arkanya, and then out at her cheering subjects, her dress billowing and sparkling in the summer sun and breeze. She leans slightly over the edge, gazing into the distance at the sea of Arkanyans at her feet, four hundred feet below. She becomes almost enthralled, seeing people who love her. She felt as close as though they were her own family, as if she knew their hearts' warmest dreams. She wipes away drool from her mouth, trying to hide the gesture with a ceremonial wave.

"People of Arkanya, as your new Rexa, it is my privilege and my honor to swear to you these next thousand years will be a time you'll never forget. A delicious time full of dreams and hope, and I can't wait to be your Rexa forever," a third and final time the crowds of Arkanya blow up in a thunderous roar of cheer and applause for their new Rexa. Separtino steps up once more for closing remarks.

"My people, rest now and get sleep, for tomorrow we shall all meet here again for the coronation of my wife!" Descendia takes his hand, kisses it, and grins to the crowd, drooling again.

# 3

## The Prophecy

Descendia, escorted by her soon-to-be husband, steps back from the balcony as the people of Arkanya go home. Families scoop up their young ones like soup from a pot, individuals cling to their groups of friends, and the occasional loners walk silently behind the popcorn spurts of commotion. All the people of Arkanya agree that this evening feels tranquil. They have much reason to rejoice after all! One thousand years of peace and their High Archon, the Rex, has found true love. What more blessed time can there be? Both peace and love pulled up a chair and brought drinks, it feels like to some. To others, despite the air of joy and peace, something feels off.

Mage Yidnar does not attend the ceremonial announcements at the Balcony of Defeat today, nor will he attend the wedding tomorrow. Something far more urgent and possibly detrimental to the entire country demands his full attention. He sweats, poring over three prophecies at once.

Suddenly, the only light in the Temple of Prophecies is that from his glowing orange hands as he uses magic to translate and decode three at once. A fair hand grabs his shoulder, startling him. In preparation for a sure battle, Yidnar turns sharply on his heel and conjures an ethereal orange sword in is hand, raising it to strike.

"Oh my goodness, darling, you must knock before coming into my temple. I was deciphering the prophecies and expected someone else," he says. Yidnar claps his hands together, making the sword disappear and conjuring a small bouquet of flowers in a swirl of glowing orange dust. It is his loving and sweet wife. She has realized he is not in bed with her asleep and has gotten up to brew him a pot of tea to relax his nerves. Yidnar and Liefadra met in a distant land far from Arkanya. They were both traveling for work, Yidnar as a traveling divination apprentice and Liefadra as an orator in the department of prophecies. All those years ago, it was love at first sight. Yidnar glanced across the room, and their eyes instantly connected, causing his hands to sweat, and he clumsily dropped all of his books before the meeting they were attending. She let out a chuckle, but her smile lingered. As Yidnar periodically glanced at her, he had not noticed a small palm-sized vine of tiny roses grow in the shape of a heart beside his left hand, and he blushed as he sat, and the lecture began. Years later, they courted, and months after that, returning home to Arkanya, they married. That is twenty-five years ago this week.

"Honey, it's nearing the vixen hour. It's time to come home," his wife, Liefadra, says as she lovingly holds his chin in her warm hands. She is a maiden who hails from the eastern Palacorn, Earth. She is tall and fair-skinned, much like her personality—strong and merciful. She is a groundskeeper for the highly venerated Heatherlyn meadows, a beautiful flower-capped series of hills as far as the eye can see. The flowers here are enchanted with magic. Should someone approach the enchanted floral meadows and pluck a single glowing sapphire-and-lilac petal, depending on the status of their heart, they will see a glimpse of either their future or their past. Shall a vile or wicked person pluck the petal, it will show what one needs to do to return to the right path and then burns away to dust.

"What is wrong, my love?" she says.

"I have discovered something of grave importance. We have no time to lose. We must go at once to the High Archon and tell him immediately. It's worse than I could possibly imagine. Liefadra, take my hand." Yidnar takes his wife's hand and immediately runs to the steps of the white marble temple, checking the moon for validation of the horrendous fate the glowing magenta and silver and black prophecy foretold to him.

"Yidnar, what happened to your hand?" she asks, running as fast as she could down the halls with her love toward the entrance.

"It's from the dark Yamirzen magic from that prophecy. Simply touching this vile orb has burned flesh from my hand. Don't fret. I can heal, but for now, it is not important." Yidnar and Liefadra run faster and faster until they finally reach the entrance of the temple and step outside to the edge of the steps, to gander at the moon. The moons are high in the sky, and there appears naught but the face of a skull. The moons are glowing a deep blood red, but the color is poorly draped over the otherwise white face as if it is bleeding or crying. The moons of Arkanya are alive. Each night and each day, they are a gauge of the safety of Arkanya. Their appearance determines the economy and whether or not war approaches. But a bleeding moon indicates that a betrayal is about to occur, a betrayal of titanic proportions that will jeopardize the entire world and all living things. Yidnar explains not just this lunar significance but also the message encrypted within the glowing magenta and black prophecy. Yidnar is terrified, and his wife is irritated he isn't telling her everything.

"Yidnar, explain to me right now," she demands. Yidnar sighs and takes out the orb once more to show her. He winces as he struggles to hold it while it stings his palm further.

"It's a foul dead language of the Yamirzen tribe, which I will not utter in these holy grounds. In our tongue it reads, 'Three babes born, each to grow to fight; two unite, each shall bring death and blight, one land to fall death to all.' It means that on this day, three people will be born, and on that same day, our world, as we know it, shall end." The horror on Yidnar's face is real. He is pale and solemn in his expressions. His brow grows high on his forehead with concern for his love as he turns around, gazing throughout the land at the vista of peaceful unknowing people lighting fires to warm their families at home. Yidnar loves his wife and his home world, and tears fall down his cheek.

"My love, as long as we have each other, we have our best, most formidable strength. Who was it who outsmarted the Lord of Malice with magic and helped the Rex defeat him a thousand years ago?" she says.

"Those days are far behind us, Liefadra. I fear what's to come may be unstoppable," Yidnar replies, bowing his head with remorse.

"We must have hope that the three proclaimed to be born will save us all." Liefadra raises his head with her kisses. "I love you to the moons," they both say, smiling. They embrace and kiss under the pink moonlight.

Mage Yidnar goes home with his wife that night and for weeks mulls over who on Arkanya can possibly be the parents of these three babes. For the life of him, he cannot determine an answer; he needs help quickly. Deep in the forests in the north of Regulusio, on the border with Earth, there lies an enormous sky-piercing willow tree, the Tree of Fayte. This tree is largely considered to be the heart of the nation. It is the purest form of all the magic in Arkanya, so pure in fact that only those who are pure of heart can lay eyes on it. Anyone selfish or overcome with greed, rage, or anything else with dark intentions cannot even see it and does not know of its existence. It is the oldest tree in all the land and continues to grow each year. Its magic is for the protection and security of the future for the people of Arkanya. Shall a person approach the Tree of Fayte, it will adapt its magic in order to aid the person most effectively, if they have the magika blood cell. Otherwise, the tree will only be able to provide guidance to the genadenz on how to cope with stressors of life to avoid depression or anxiety.

Yidnar begins packing a bag for his weeklong journey to the Tree of Fayte. In order to do this, one cannot merely teleport to the tree; her usage must be earned by honest work, and part of that means to travel the old-fashioned way.

"Are you sure you don't want me to join you? It's such a long journey to travel on foot," Liefadra asks as she fills his bag with home-baked foods for his journey. She prepares his favorite meals for his journey: corn bread, dumplings, and fried poultry sandwiches. Whenever an Arkanyan Creytian makes a pilgrimage to the Tree of Fayte, all who notices know not to disturb them. So for Yidnar, he needn't worry about spectators wasting his time with conversation, for none of them does. For days, he marches slowly and solely on his way, northwest toward the great tree. He wants to validate his translations, to double-check his work. He also wants clarity on the three babes born.

At last, seven days after his journey began (needing to stop periodically to camp for food and water), he arrives at the roots of the amazing, gargantuan tree. The roots react to his presence, untwisting and writhing and spreading apart, revealing the face of the Tree of Fayte. A face carved to be part of the tree itself comes alive and greets him. He is amazed, slightly fearful, and awestruck all at once in the presence of the Tree.

"Welcome, Yidnar, son of Atmar," the tree speaks.

Yidnar does not expect that. "Greetings, Tree of Fayte. I come to you for aid, and the safety of my people." Yidnar takes out the Propheta Fior and holds it up to the tree. "I have discovered a prophecy which foretells of three babes to be born sometime this year, and on that day, the end of the world also comes. Who are the three babies? How can I protect my people?" asks Yidnar. The tree grows angry in close proximity to the hissing orb.

"The Propheta Fior of which you speak was correctly translated by yourself. It shall come to pass. However, it is not the end times. It is the death of everything as we know it, but that does not mean there can't be an existence of which we currently know nothing," the tree cryptically answers. Yidnar writes down the tree's answers for contemplation later. "As for the three babes, they are your creychildren." Yidnar looks confused. *Creychildren,* a term which here means godchildren.

"That can't be. I do not have creychildren," says the mage.

"You will, soon. And once you do, all will be as it should and can never be undone," the tree finishes. As it speaks its final word, the roots writhe and twist again, this time closing like the curtain of a stage production show. Yidnar finishes his notes from the interaction and teleports back home in a whisp of red and yellow leaves.

In the flash of nature and light, he returns home to his loving but stressed and worrying wife, shares what he learned, and explains that everything depends on the future creychildren.

"But honey, no one we know is pregnant," she replies.

"I know, but we must have faith. The tree never lies. Let's keep what the Tree said to ourselves for now we must protect all that we can. We are more at risk than the rest. Now we must alert the High Archon and inform him of the Propheta Fior with the justification of the Tree of Fayte." Liefadra nods in agreement, takes her husband's arm, and suddenly, on the ground by their feet, Yidnar uses magic to teleport them both to the Rex's Great Hall. A meeting of the highest urgency regarding national homeland safety is called for. Ethereal and shimmering orange green and amber leaves rustle and swirl faster and faster around them. In a bright-orange flash, they are gone before the leaves settle.

With a bright-orange flash, Yidnar and Liefadra appear, walking swiftly with purpose and intent down the gilded Great Hall. A few stray magical orange red and amber leaves from Yidnar's magic fall slowly to the ground behind them.

"Your Arkanisty, we wish to discuss the safety of Arkanya with you at once," Yidnar calls out, with his long-aged robes flowing behind him. His left hand held the hissing and magenta-glowing orb magenta Yamirzen and his love in the other hand.

The captain of the Rex's personal guard approaches them from the shadows beyond the gates. His dull and weathered armor hides his face efficiently, but Yidnar knows this man personally.

"Bonmal, I seek the Rex at once. You must hurry. All is at stake. Tell him that Sayjet is here." Sayjet is Yidnar's one of many nicknames, this one referencing how the two of them met a thousand years ago.

Deep in the genadenz non-magical forest to the south in Denebia, Yidnar in his youth had come to read some ancient tomes and enjoy the quiet arboretum sanctuary. As it happened, another young lad Separtino had also come to enjoy just the same. Each day, the two found each other and eventually struck up conversation and became the closest of friends. Yidnar had not yet turned fifteen and had not yet sworn allegiance to the protection of Arkanya. Likewise, Separtino had not yet discovered the potion, which for a genadenz grants long life.

Remember that potions, though created for a unique single intent, operates unpredictably for the genadenz. Separtino was born without the magika blood cell. His parents do not love each other and do not have a belief in the afterlife. Not meeting the criteria for his own magika blood cell, all he can do is drink potions and use runes.

Bonmal narrows his glare at the visitors; his trust has dried up. "Prove to me you are who you claim."

"Show me your right hand," Yidnar replies. Bonmal takes off one obsidian-armored gauntlet, exposing his dark-skinned hand. Yidnar's eyes illuminate orange in the shadows, and he can read the man's palm. "You were born in the mountains in the north, abandoned as a child. You were raised by beasts and Arkanyans alike, granting you your powerful unique spells of—"

"That's enough, thank you. Follow me," Bonmal quickly dons his gauntlet and guides them to the Rex's chamber. Down the stone halls, the lighting grows darker and darker until Yidnar snaps fingers in his right hand and a small but helpful flame appears, like a torch. Left and right the hallway twists until finally they arrive at massive golden doors with a great big amethyst as a knocker. Bonmal knocksd on the door, and it opens. Yidnar places the now hissing and whispering Yamirzen prophecy on the Rex's desk and explains his findings, but surprisingly, to no avail. The Rex stands up with frustration and irritation.

"How dare you claim that my hard work of a thousand years for peace is all for nothing! You dare even further to claim ridiculously that these rhyming child's poems are somehow tied to my wife? You're a damned fool, Sayjet! You're old, and your magic has withered away, much like your gray whore of a wife beside you. You're lucky I don't banish you for insolence and treason," Separtino roars.

"I am not trying to demean you! I'm trying to warn you! There is a threat more powerful than anything I've ever sensed before, Rex! Look at my hand! I can't even touch this magic without boiling the skin to the bone! You look at this and tell me we should ignore it! I have sworn allegiance and devoted my entire life to the protection of your kingdom! We *must* prepare!"

"FOR WHAT, YOU FOOL?" Rex shouts. Separtino has never called his oldest friend and ally a fool before.

"For the end of the world," Descendia slithers her way into the ignored front door and sits down at the nearest chair. She is wearing a sparkling black-and-purple crystal-studded dress with a high multi-pointed collar as if it has daggers. She laughs at the notion of the apocalypse and mocks Yidnar's claims with style and propensity for maintaining both a grin and a demeanor of discontent. "Shall I get you a gold star for your efforts?" She laughs again, louder this time.

"If you won't take any action, I will. I have sworn my life to the protection of this land, our home, and by Drakulogons, I will! Take my hand, Liefadra." Yidnar reaches out a hand but feels only the chill night air embrace his fingers.

Descendia has, in mere milliseconds, cast three spells. The first freezes time for all in the room. The second makes her appear so close to Yidnar and Liefadra that their noses almost touch. The third, sadly, conjures her fingers into blades, and she digs her hands into the heart of Yidnar's true love and wife. "And she lived unhappily ever after!" Descendia mocked the murder of the innocent Liefadra.

Yidnar, despite the magical freezing of time, immediately cries profusely, screaming "No!" as loud as he possibly can, trying with every spell he can think of to free them from the curse, but it is too late. Just as the witch disappears with her husband, Liefadra's lifeless body, still holding the fear on her face, falls to black ash on the floor, and Yidnar vanishes. Yidnar vanishes with a damp face of old tears and a heart full of anguish.

# 4

## Crowning Misery

Mage Yidnar teleports away from the Rex's chambers and weeps for his losses. He loses his best friend, the first person who understood him from centuries ago, throws away his friendship as if it were rotten food; it confuses Yidnar as to why their camaraderie is so easily tossed aside. To him, the number of good memories have vastly outweighed the indifferent or the bad. The pain of losing such a friend is great and piercing.

It is nothing when compared to the loss of his wife and any hope for a family, for it is not just his wife he has lost in Liefadra but his family. She was his chance at long-term happiness, he thought, at starting a family of his own and one day leave behind a legacy for the protection of Arkanya and the upkeep of the ancient linguistic arkane arts.

Yidnar wipes away his tears, lifts his head up, and grabs the hissing cursed prophecy from his nightstand. With a snap of his fingers, his presence is replaced by a wisp of rustling, billowing trails of leaves. The board is set; the game has begun.

Meanwhile, at the Temple of Prophecies, the Rex has gathered as many citizens as he can inside the grounds of the temple. Only the lucky few will be able to witness the coronation ceremony in the same room as the archdeacon and the Rex and his wife, Descendia. One by one, the peace-loving families and individuals of Arkanya enter the auditorium and take their seats, anxiously awaiting the ceremony to begin. They are excited! This is a glittering, noble, and social event, one filled with a reunion of long not seen familiar faces, as well as music, fireworks, live music provided by the High Archon's band, and food prepared by the best chefs in all of Leonulia. Made with the freshest of ingredients, cooked with the finest appliances, and prepared with passion, the food can be smelled miles away, filling the noses and hearts of all who came with joy.

"Silence! The sacred coronation of our Rexa begins now!" cries the archdeacon. He is an older gentleman, with as much faith as a saint. This is to be his final call, however. He longs to reunite with his family and live out his retirement days at home quietly.

The band music intensifies as the Rex marches down the aisle in his most glamorous and ceremonial robe made from materials from each of his Palacorn. Every fiber of clothing represents his country. The medals on his chest represent the unprecedented years of peace and the victory over the First Battle with the infamous Lord of Malice, Kalypto. The medals clang together in their gold metal state but also clash in their opposite contexts, war and peace side by side on his armored breastplate, knocking together like warning bells until finally the medal for peace, unbeknownst to himself, breaks free from its clasp and falls to the ground.

Mage Yidnar appears in a subtle wisp of leaves flowing and hides near the back of the room, waiting to aid in service should anything he is suspicious of reveal to be true.

"All rise for the ascending Descendia of the South Mountains," the archdeacon announces the coming of the future Rexa of Arkanya. All eyes and heads swivel, as if by pressing a button, to her direction, and there is an audible gasp from the audience, for her attire is interesting.

She clads herself in a simple black velvet dress fitted at the waist and flared out from her legs like a big Gothic bell. The skirt, which spills to the floor hiding her feet, is also sharply pleated, making the skirt section look like it is clad in tentacles and webbed. The bodice, like the skirt, is a deep, dark black, like obsidian shimmering with diamond dust speckling and sparkling upon it. The sleeves are a blood-red sheer fabric and the collar stands up jagged like a bat wing. As soon as she enters, a violent thunderstorm begins outside. Thunder erupting set the rhythm for each left footstep. She walks toward her crown, gazing with the same disturbing grimace, drooling at the crowds bowing down on their knees to her. As she approaches her ultimate goal, the fates of all in this room will be sealed forever. In fact, the fate of even the author is sealed, as is the door, the only exit. The band is silent, but the children's choir sings a hymn that is both chilling and sweet at the same time, the lyrics calling for protection of their souls and their homes. They are harmonizing in high notes as if they are pleading for mercy while also celebrating a coronation. For you see, all generations of Arkanyans are in this room, but not just any Arkanyans, only the genadenz.

The archdeacon carries on the ceremony; however, everything stops shortly after. As soon as he arrives at the part in his long-ago memorized script to ask her to vow and affirm her oath to protect, love, and serve the country of Arkanya, she begins coughing into hysterics. A few gentlemen offer her drink and food to clear her throat, and still another offers medical attention, all of which she refuses.

A bright and heavy fog of magenta haze encircles the woman, and the presence of this pink cloud causes everyone to fall to their hands and knees coughing, and some have internal bleeding, not being able to take so much toxicity from the Yamirzen magic billowing out of the "woman." The crowds scream if they can while others succumb to the shock and pain of her dark, forbidden magic. The grounds of Arkanya begin to rumble and shake. The land of Arkanya, being alive with magic, rejects the atrocity that is now exposed in the Temple of Prophecies. They scream because not only is it rare to have such powerful magic, but it is the destruction of their sanity to see the woman they all approved of just a day ago now reveals herself clearly to be a demon of some kind... But that's just it as well—she has dark magic. How on Arkanya can you have *dark* magic if you only get the blood cell for it when your parents truly loved each other and believed in an afterlife? Things don't add up, yet there she is.

You see, this is not a mere woman whom the people of Arkanya once loved. She is, in fact, the mistress of Kalypto, the Devourer of Hope, Massacara. Her eyes are the first to change as lightning flashes and rain comes down in sheets and buckets. Her eyes boil like eggs on a fire and drip out of her skull; her skin forms a spider web of cracks that becomes darker and more refined as the seconds pass until they burst open like seams in clothing and a thick disgusting, stinking mud-like liquid spills out over the floor. When she stops screaming, she opens her eyes to the crowd, revealing black volcanic rocks with glowing lava appearing behind tiny cracks within. She writhes in pain and duress as her vile spells wear off, revealing piece by piece who she really is. Her hair is stringy, like a dirty old mop; her skin is the color of mold; her hands are naught but dagger blades; her jaw is shaped like a V instead of a normal U; her back is hunched; and her neck is short. The crowds of innocent and trapped Arkanyans are screaming with terror as they see the disturbing and terrifying monster crack open the shell of the body the people knew her as, revealing her true form: this grotesque witch. The innocent audience members begin clamoring and running to the only entrance and exit of this building, but it is far too late.

Descendia slaps the archdeacon with a dagger hand, slicing off his head and stealing the crown from his grasp. The amethyst crown levitates into the air and nestles on her head as she opens her horrible, molten eyes. She looks around the room, smiling and laughing in her hunched stance, drooling profusely at the sight of such a buffet. The Rexa can no longer control herself. The question is what can she no longer control? The crowned witch is guided by her cadaverous hands that are so desperately reaching out ahead for something. She almost loses her balance, leaving the raised platform and the massacred corpse of the shell she once wore. She stretches her hands out as far as she can, trying to sense as much as she can to find the rawest meal. Suddenly, she narrows in on one particular married couple. Time all around her slows to one sixteenth the normal rate. All the enchanted and blessed Heatherlyn flowers wilted, blackened, and died. She places one hand on the man's back and another on his chest.

"Who are you, vile witch? What do you want?" the man cries, trying to be as brave as he can. The horrendous, drooling, molding witch smiles and laughs. She leans in, touching her crooked nose to his, her molten eyes glowing in the lava cracks like dying coals for a campfire. The man can see that random sections of her flesh have rotted away, exposing veins and bones.

"You dream to one day raise a family in a world where everything is certain, where you can never be without purpose. A place you actually love because there's one small thing that would ruin your family if they ever knew." She smiles and glances at his wife. "He blames the child for the death of his dreams! YOU FOOL! It is not her, my dear man, it is *me*!" she shrieks and cackles hysterically. Lightning flashes once more exposing how skin-and-bone skinny she is. With that, her butcher's hands glow magenta and hum with a powerful curse. She lunges one hand deep into the heart of his wife, causing him to scream in heartache and agony and fear. She cackles maniacally and then lunges both of her cursed hands into his own heart, lifting him off the floor and smiling at him widely. "One lesson for you before you go sweetie! Hope is a treacherous vile trait, which only brings you *pain*!" She opens her mouth far wider than any normal human and devours the man whole, crunching her mouth, savoring the taste of his hopes and dreams, her mouth glowing blue as she consumes the purest form of hope from the man's own heart. The people of Arkanya who are trapped inside the temple shriek and scream in traumatizing fear watching and hearing this demon literally eat hope, and she searches for her next meal. People are confused as they don't understand why she is targeting so randomly, and there is nowhere for anyone to go.

# 5

## The Devourer of Hope

She moves onto the next family of victims for her long-awaited meal. Massacara, as she is more truthfully known, has not feasted on the juicy, tender, fragile hopes of the innocent in an age. From the moment she entered the Temple of Prophecies to begin her coronation, she is delighted beyond reckoning to begin eating, tempted by her favorite treat all around her. Like a child in a candy store, looks around the room smiling and drooling. She imagines how deliciously exhilarating each vulnerable sliver of hope will taste.

She moves to another man, then another family, and another, and again another! The Witch of Death is too busy feasting to realize something else is happening. It is too quick even if she isn't eating hopes and dreams, for time is of the essence. In a flash so sudden of his orange magic, she barely skips a beat, wiping the glowing purity of hope from her jaws before continuing, laughing and cackling amidst the screams of horror and thunder.

Yidnar appears back at the Palace of the Falls to alert the Rex that his wife has, nay, is currently committing the highest form of treason, killing innocent civilians in the vilest way imaginable, though technically, she is only eating their hope. What Yidnar left too early to grimly realize is, she hasn't murdered a single person. Yes, she robbed them entirely of their hope, but it is they themselves who, without any hope at all, elect to do themselves in—a truth that makes even the flowers on the walls weep as if they are shedding the morning dew to honor the fallen, wilting despite their enchanted glow.

Yidnar races up the stone spiral staircase up to the entrance of the Rex's chambers. Bonmal is on guard, of course, but neither of them pays the other any mind for duty took priority. Bonmal is one of the most revered, respected, and dangerous of all watches: the watch of the Potion of Nauz. This potion has no description other than its crafted intended use: to disintegrate the magika blood cell from any magakos who broke any of the three laws of magic. Due to the potion's highly volatile nature, it is protected and guarded by both magical and non-magical methods, complete with a magakos soldier, Bonmal, and his companion, Broque, a genadenz, to keep watch.

"What do you think is happening at the coronation ceremony at the temple today, Bon?" asks Broque. He is a very buff yet agile man hailing from the peaceful and fruitful lands of Acamaro in the southeast. Tall, tan, and broad from growing up on the farms, Broque enjoys quiet times reading books with his wife, teaching his three kids how to work certain tools on the farms, and harvesting the fruits, vegetables, and meats for the country to enjoy and nourish with. Bonmal is a harder man. He is of average height but much leaner and has a large head, not exaggerated, just slightly bigger than normal. He hails from the south near the mountains in Denebia. The two of them met in their youth attending the same temple for their faith and frequenting hiking trips in the same locations throughout the lands over the years.

"I don't know, but I bet the food is amazing!" Bonmal rubs his stomach. He hasn't eaten in a few hours, longer than normal for him.

"Anything would be better than guard rations!" Broque jests. They both laugh and then hear Yidnar running fiercely up the stairs. Bonmal raises a hand for them both to be silent, and he watches his friend.

Yidnar uses magic in a counterclockwise wave to magically erase the door from existence and steps through.

"Separtino? Separtino! Descendia is much worse than I feared. You must come with me!" Yidnar smartly leaves out the details that this man's wife and everyone's Rexa has begun tearing the hope from his people and eating it like candy.

Separtino is gazing into a crystal ball, watching his wife do what Yidnar tried to warn him about.

"I never thought she'd be capable of even a quarter of this, Yidnar, I loved her so much. How could I be so stupid?" he cries.

"We can still stop this treachery, end this darkness before it's too late!"

"I know now is so inappropriate because my people need me, but you don't understand, Sayjet. She was everything I wanted in a wife. We went on adventures together. We made decisions together as a couple. We shared the same beliefs, or so I thought, at least. I am going to need some time. She was my love. I don't know if I'll ever marry again." Separtino weeps for the loss of his one true love. She came into his life at a time when he wanted love the most, a time when his country is celebrating a thousand years of peace.

But there is more for Yidnar; he can tell that this is not natural love for the two has only known each other a day. This is another one of the witch's curses. Separtino's eyes only up close had a slight visible tinge of magenta light—Massacra's magic color. But why will she need him to love her? What else is she planning?

"You are not stupid. Love is such a fleeting thing, whenever we are blessed enough to feel it, we want it to be true and last forever. But sometimes the people we love don't love us back. Sometimes the people we love just want to use us. She used you, Separtino. She used you to block my efforts in preventing her carnage and get to the heart of Arkanya with your approval. But let's not worry about that now. Take my arm!" Yidnar consoles his best friend. Separtino hugs him and weeps onto his shoulder.

The moment Rex takes his arm is the precise moment the two of them lands back inside the temple, and there is absolute chaos. Massacara has eaten about 375 of the 600 guests, and the rest are clamoring around the only exit.

"Yidnar, what in the blazes do we do?"

"You love her, right? Distract her, and I will work on saving the people. Be quick! And do *not* believe a word she says about anything!"

The rest of the evening at the temple becomes an exodus to swiftly flee from The Devourer of Hope, to safety with Yidnar grabbing as many civilians as he can, "poofing" them out group by group. After a handful of trips, Yidnar appears back in the temple to an entirely empty auditorium. Empty, yes, but when only the living are counted. Littering the ground like poppies at a war memorial are the massacred corpses of families.

He snaps fingers and summons an orb of light to follow him and guide him to the rest of the people. He runs after the orb ahead of him and is more and more confused about what is happening. Suddenly, it dawns on him as he runs down the temple stairs and toward the cliff edge near the river leading back to the Palace of the Falls. Sure enough, his dark thought is right. Massacara has magic and has thrown every last living person a thousand feet off the cliff edge to their deaths, but not before tearing away all of their hopes and dreams. Their beautiful hopes for a warmer future lies like gross scraps after a poor-mannered beast is finished mauling its prey glowing pure in their goodness, a beautiful blue all over the cliff edge. One scene shows the sad dead bodies of a reunited family after three children returns home from distant schooling, hugging together as one at home; another shows a father reuniting with his estranged son, hugging instead of having shouting matches; another shows a daughter graduating from school and making enough money to save her sick mother; the list goes on. Yidnar weeps for the beautiful dreams these people of Arkanya were so close to having but now never can. He holds his head with mounting stress and fear and wants so badly for this all to be over, but he knows it has not even begun. He looks over his left shoulder and sees a bright pink light flash at the Balcony of Defeat, at the top of the Palace of the Falls, and his somber expression turns into a fed-up frown. As he storms away from the cliff edge in the blink of an eye, he is replaced by rustling leaves and teleports to the balcony.

Appearing with a loud thunderclap with orange lightning, he yells, "Coward! Fight me! Fight me now, witch!" He storms around the Rex's chambers looking for the two, but sees nothing and no one. And then in the distance, directly on the balcony, sees them. They are saying their goodbyes, and so Yidnar attempts to hide as best he can with magic thankful no one heard his entrance.

Massacara and Separtino are dancing together, with the corpses of her victims below. The jackal moon is now entirely blood red, and Yidnar watches, hoping they are just saying goodbye, but is ready to fight if needed.

*'Massacara looks like her "pretty" self again this time for Separtino, no doubt,'* Yidnar thinks.

"I love you, Descendia. I love you so much with—" Separtino is interrupted by her finger on his lips as they slowly dance the foxtrot.

"Every beat of your heart? I know. So does mine for you, my cherished one." They continue dancing together, drifting in their balletic movements closer to the edge of the balcony. She keeps his back to the moon and the water below.

"I will be your protector for all my years, and after I'm gone, my spirit will cherish and defend you from any harm, my darling." He dips his wife and seals his promise with a red rose from his sleeve and a kiss. "We will be happy until—" Again he is cut off.

"Until the end of... Arkanya!" The vile molding and rotting witch leaned in for a kiss, slowly revealing her true face to him.

"No! No! It cannot be!" The Rex feels betrayed and is pierced through his heart by her lies and her daggered hand.

"Love and hope are hollow and false, you fool," she hisses like a viper. "Tell me, sweetie, what does your heart hope for?" She backs him up to the railing nearest the edge of the balcony, with their noses touching and her periodically kissing him to keep him quiet. "What does your heart dream of more than anything?" Massacara's eyes immediately run black like coals with lava seeping through the cracks, her hands flash bright magenta, and she lets out a deafening cackle as the balcony crumbles where Separtino stood moments ago, and he falls, heartbroken, crying, and alone to his watery death a thousand feet below. Massacara crawls out of her cadaverous shell and, with her hunch, walks to the edge, watching him splash into the river and down the falls. Yidnar magically mutes himself as he screams in emotional distress, watching his childhood best friend murdered, betrayed, and defeated all at once. She cackles maniacally and conjures a bolt of lightning to strike his corpse. She cackles once more, then like a hunter, immediately stares directly into Yidnar's eyes and says, "Separtino today, Arkanya tomorrow," and vanishes in a disgusting explosion of black tar.

# 6

## The Beginning of the End: Kalypto

A hundred thousand years ago in Arkanya, there lived a strong but arrogant magakos male and a genadenz female, Horatio and Nervana. They lived in a modest cottage deep in the woods past the Heatherlyn meadows far out west in Denebia. The two had been married for six years but had grown apart tremendously. Daily, Horatio would beat his wife almost to the point of unconsciousness. He hated her as much as he loved himself.

"You'll never amount to anything, you lousy piece of shite! You got that? Shite is better than you, scum," he shouted as he beat her more, yelling louder drowning out her cries for help.

"You're a fool! You're a miserable, pathetic fool, and no one loves you! No one cares for you, and no one ever will because you're not worth the time or effort it takes to care for someone!" He hated her as much as he possibly could and vowed to remind her at every opportunity how despised she was. He was so intent on showing her his hatred that he would go out of his way to find new ways to torment and torture the poor sweet woman. She had no magic of her own, and so she was at a terrible disadvantage, but it was the love of her son that kept her smiling despite the hell she lived. Her baby boy was the root of the smallest glimmer of light in her life. Horatio loved his son almost as much as he hated his wife, for how could something as vile as a "brainless cretin like you give birth to a strapping young babe like him? You're not capable of it! Who did you sleep with? Who did you cheat on me with?" Horatio falsely accused his wife of being unfaithful though the Drakulogon knew she would have had reason if it were true.

She lay there, having collapsed with him whipping her back. Despite the pain, she prayed to Adonai, "Dear Lord of Arkanya, please let him see the folly of his actions and of his words. Let him allow himself to love me and have mercy on me, please." She prayed as hard as she could and chose to love and protect her son more than harbor any hatred for her horrendous husband. Despite his accusations, Horatio saw himself in the babe's face already and knew in his mind that was his son. Their son was already seven years old, but you would never know it because the young lad spent every second of every minute of every day in bed.

"One day, young Kalypto, people will bow to your presence, and you will go down in history as the most memorable wizard in the world, the greatest sorcerer who ever lived!" Horatio kissed his smiling son's forehead.

Horatio was a complicated man. He hated his Gypsy wife for believing in an afterlife, thinking as a man of magic and arkane maths that she was nuts. As a result, he wanted his son to have a better life, one he could not provide. So he ran through the forest for weeks, procuring the rarest of ingredients: the wings from a luminescent moth in the caves near the Eirini River, a bottle of sap from the deepest root of the Tree of Fayte in the north in Regulusio, a petal from the flowers of the Heatherlyn meadows, and lastly, powder from the ground down enchanted gems in the south mountains. Together with high temperatures, he created a rare curse, the curse of the second life. The potion Horatio then placed a hex over to have the potion never deplete and never weaken in potency. He connected tubes from the cauldron to a needle and stuck them in the arms and chest of his sleeping son. As the molten liquid curse of a second life began injecting into his son's bloodstream, Kalypto had a completely different life.

As long as the curse was injected, the boy would never be the wiser, never wake up, and never experience anything in the real world.

Kalypto's cursed life was one of much more happiness. They lived in a bustling city in the Leonulia region where he excelled in academia, was critically acclaimed for his artistic and athletic abilities, popular among his plethora of friends, and the founder of many clubs in the community. His parents both loved each other dearly, and they did everything as a family: take vacations to the picturesque beaches of Earth, historic battleground tours of Regulusio, voyages on ships around the oceans in Denebia; ate the most delicious and fresh feasts and attended the most lavish of festivals in Acamaro; and they grew their religious faith in the breathtakingly beautiful Temple of Prophecies in Leonulia. It was a wonderful life filled with charm, warm love and care from his friends and family, wisdom and lessons learned from his time at university, and he developed his magical combat and constructive skills tremendously so at the School of the Arkane near the Palace of the Falls. Kalypto was a paragon of charisma, positive energy, light, and above all, ambition. Everyone wanted to be like him, and he had the world in his hands it seemed.

One day, Horatio and Nervana went at it again. What started out as an argument led to something far darker.

"How dare you drug our son with your concoctions from hell! Have you any idea what you're dabbling in? Do you know what could happen to us if the Rex finds out what kinds of spells these are? What is the matter with you!" Nervana ran around the house ducking from the swords that Horatio was heaving through the air, all of them glowing bright red, the color of his rage and magic.

"You hollow imbecile! You don't even understand nor comprehend the very language you speak, yet you attempt to accuse me of harming our son? I've made him safer than you ever could, you damned insane wastrel!"

"The only thing you'll ever make safe is your own love of yourself, you arrogant gas bag! And how in the oblivion you can love yourself is beyond me! Your soul is as black as tar, your heart is as small as your toes and—" She was cut off. Only this time not by someone else's words. One of the enormous blades Horatio was throwing out of rage at his wife sliced dead center through her chest, slicing her body right in between her lungs and grazing her heart. She tried to still stand and disconnect her son's curse, but she so quickly lost control of her limbs and thoughts and collapsed with the tubes in her hands, tears streaming down her face. As she collapsed, she rolled to the side of her wound, bringing with her the curse tubes, and falling onto the shelf with the cauldron. Horatio saw this and used his magic to shield the bottles of ingredients so he could make more after killing her, he hoped. Yes, he cared more about his precious magic than his own wife. Her deadweight smashed the old table, tore the tubes out of their sockets from the cauldron and from her son's arms and chest. Her act of true love broke the spell that was maintaining the potency and amount of curse potion. With a flash and pulse of white light, that spell was shattered. The pulse threw everything loose in the room like a great gust of hurricane winds. When she hit the floor, she tried to speak but was choking on her own blood. Horatio ran over to her when he saw her go down. Horatio got to his dying wife's body, and she had one last message for him.

"You are the true cursed soul. No matter what you do to anyone else, you are cursed with never feeling love for anyone but yourself." She took so long to say this that she died exhaling the last word. This was too much for Horatio to take.

By this time Kalypto's world was collapsing all around him—buildings and skyscrapers toppled over like the cardboard props they were, and people melted and boiled away into nothing. He ran around the world screaming with trauma and fear and immense confusion. Everything and everyone he knew peeled away like the skin of a lemon, leaving only the sour truth.

"What in the hell is happening? What is wrong with everyone?" He grabbed hold of anything he could to prevent himself from fainting, but he was also enraged by why this was happening. Who was causing it? He was ready to kill to defend the people he loved, the world he loved, the very life he knew.

Finally, he too began melting and boiling away, and as he screamed, he woke up to cold, harsh reality. His eyes focused, and he was screaming more, not having any idea where he was, who he was, or anything. He jumped out of bed and looked around the room, screaming senseless things, thinking so many things at once: *My entire life was a lie. What the hell actually happened to me? Where did everyone go? What is this place? Who am I?* He was violently clumsy. He was no fool, though. He crawled over to the desk with the destroyed cauldron and examined the empty bottles for their original ingredients and understood what spell had been made. Furious, he looked at the tubes from the cauldron to the bed he just left and put two and two together. He was seething with rage, so angry his skin turned red as his blood boiled inside him. He turned around again and saw his mother. Even in his fake life she looked the same, only with less blood. He wept and moaned in sadness and agony for the loss of his loving mother, held her in his arms, and cried into her arms, kissing her head, trying to wake her up to no avail.

"My son," Horatio called out, wanting to explain everything.

Kalypto stood up shaking and falling back to his knees.

"You killed my mother! You monster! You fowl, deranged demon! You're dead to me! You tore away my life! You ate my life's happiness!"

"No son, I can explain. I did all this to protect you. I hated your stupid mother and wanted to give you a life I know I never could—a happy one with a loving family!"

"So you cursed me with a lie? You damned, insane fool. I'll kill you! You killed my mother! You consumed my entire life! All of it was fake!"

Kalypto engaged in hand-to-hand combat, beating the life out of his father to a pulp. Horatio could not get a swing in as his son was too furious and pumped with curses, adrenaline, and rage and vengeance. Kalypto punched as hard as he could upward against the bottom of his father's chin, shattering his spine and killing him before he hit the floor, but that was not the end. Kalypto tore out the blade that killed his mother and hacked away at his father until he was doused from head to toe in his father's blood, spitting gulps of his father's blood and screaming with rage in every swing. There was nothing but blood and bones left from his father. It was so fast there was not even a scream.

Kalypto screamed once more, finally stopping and looking at the gruesome sight of the death of his family, the death of his dreams, and the death of the life he never would have, the death of the fake life he never had, and the death of any hope for a second life.

He collapsed to the floor in such trauma he could barely concentrate. He looked up at the sky and thought to himself, *Happiness is a lie, an illusion which must never be felt. Had I never felt happiness, I wouldn't have lost my family, my life, and my dreams. I'll never be happy again.* He wept, still dripping in blood and scarred for the remainder of his days.

Kalypto stood up screaming as tears mixed with blood in his eyes and spawning terrible magical diseases. He drank a bottle of potion to try to heal the wound, but as a genadenz, the potion had an adverse effect, melting the skin off his body; he screamed harder now, his voice raspy with such yelling and shrieking. Remember that magic in Arkanya only worked correctly with magakos people, and Kalypto was not a magakos. Magic also had moral repercussions. Was his father an innocent man? Not in the slightest. Did he deserve to be completely ground to juice by his son? Absolutely not. He drank another, which disintegrated his organs one by one, and it killed him. He too let out his last breath as he broke his jaw with a potion bottle and landed facedown in the cauldron. He swallowed before coughing up blood and drank every potion from his father's collection. The shrieks and screams from the pain of having his muscle tissues, veins, hair, and most of his body burn off to ash on the floor. His screams echoed to silence as Kalypto lay in a smoldering pile of remains. The magical curse and vile combination of Yamirzen potions resurrected Kalypto though in the most terrible and horrifying form: a billowing, blowing, and smoky collection of sulfur-smelling black fog, with only obsidian-clad claws for hands and a horned skull for a face. There lit a fire inside his skull, flames billowing out of the angry-looking eye sockets and razor-sharp, fang-clad jaws. In a black and silver explosion of Yamirzen magic, all throughout Arkanya an earthquake shuddered, creating the South Mountains and the cliff edges in the north at the foot of the Palace of the Falls. The Lord of Malice, the King of Wrath, the Cleaver of Happiness, Kalypto, was born.

You may be wondering how someone as unhinged and vengeful as Kalypto can have the magika blood cell since you can only have it if your parents fall in true love and they both believe in an afterlife, right? Well, magic, like life, is not black or white. Kalypto's parents felt something as deep as love for each other, only it wasn't love; it was utter hatred. Also, the mother believed in an afterlife, a peaceful place where one can experience true happiness if they live a good life. His father did not only believe in such things but also thought anyone who does is "dumber than Nervana," as he'd say. As a result, the magic in Kalypto was born from their conflict, their hatred for each other, and their contrasting belief in the absolute truth: life after death. Therefore, Kalypto's innate magic is the darkest and most combustible form of Yamirzen magic ever known to exist in all of Arkanya.

# 7

## Hope and Happiness

Yidnar has just, in a matter of only twelve hours, lost his wife, and now he has lost his childhood friend. This witch that has descended upon Arkanya has brought with her darker forces of the Yamirzen powers than anyone has ever seen. To use magic in such a way that she can personify or solidify and make tangible the intangible—hope—and then consume it, leaving their bodies massacred? Not only is it a disgusting act to be forced to bear witness to, but it is also one of the most heinous magical deeds one could accomplish with such dark power.

Yidnar now knows exactly who it is the hissing Propheta Fior is referring to in its phrase "Two unite, each shall bring death and blight." It is not some stranger no one has met named Descendia, whatever the hell that name means. It is instead Massacara who has descended upon Arkanya. But who in blazes is she to unite with? Surely she alone is a threat enough. What else can happen to Arkanya?

After Massacara defeats Separtino on the destroyed Balcony of Defeat, she flies back to deep in the Schrie Mountains. As she teleports into a whirling magenta-and-black cloud, her disgusting thick, black tar drips and pours muck all over the world. She soars high into the sky, and people below are screaming, trapped in her tar, now unable to move. As she passes, she snaps her dagger fingers and lights them ablaze, cackling as more innocent people perishes painfully. Where is she going?

Her course zeroes in on one particular mountain, not the tallest but not the shortest, and no, 'tis not the most average either. It is but a random mountain against which she smashes through and plunges ever deeper into the Arkanya crust, all the while being surrounded by horrible, twisted fowl creatures the likes of which none has ever been so unfortunate to witness, skeletons with roaches as eyes, swords as arms, and spiders crawling wherever they so choose. These mindless, evil beings are the Skrall, a demented hybrid monster of varying types, all of whom have pledged eternity to serve their Rexa.

Finally, she reaches the very bottom, and her gaseous state piles and billows atop itself, slowly transforming into the hideous and now obese monster of a witch she is. Fat she has become after her more than satisfying feast upon the dreams and hopes of innocents earlier. Ahead of her is the evilest being in all of creation. His very name struck so much fear that it is considered part of the lost cursed language, never to be praised. His presence has made Massacara herself completely incapable of moving. She can feel everything, hear and see everything, but she cannot even blink, let alone inhale at times. There are no plants or animals down here in the fiery pits, but if there are, they will turn black, not with death but with sadness. It is none other than Kalypto himself in his hazy clouds of deceit and blackness cloaking his obsidian claws each the size of a wagon, crowned by his juicy, gruesome, ferocious horned skull for a head. Inside the head is a magical fire, which though currently is blue could change color depending on his rage or spells being used.

The Cleaver of Peace turns around to gaze upon the witch and congratulates her.

"Congratulations, young witch. You have done well. Thou hath only existed in the palace for a day or two, and yet hundreds you have already felled. Well done!" With every word the Lord of Malice speaks, the mountains rumble and tremble. His voice is deep and raspy as if he has been screaming all day, and his throat is coarse, though, of course, he has no throat.

"This is nothing. When my plans are complete, I'll eat all the hope in Leonulia! The stupid Palacorn that claims to worship the

Drakulogon but can't even protect one little temple! The liars! The imbeciles!" The witch hysterically cackles and laughs viciously.

"Silence, you fool! You will not consume a single additional life until *my plans* have begun. Then, my dear, you'll feast upon the entire world. Now, how does that sound?" Kalypto grins in his horned and menacing skull. "In three months' time, it will be the fifteenth Idamay, which means that the moon will be full, and then, then I can cast the ultimate Yamirzen spell, Jigocrugya, to turn the land into hell. This world makes us believe that happiness is real. At the start, it always feels real, but it's an illusion. It's a lie as hollow as a dead, petrified tree, and only the incompetent chooses to believe otherwise! *There is no joy! None!* There cannot be, for it is not true. It is not real. Therefore, Massacara, we *show the pathetic mongrels that their entire lives are naught but ash and fire*! The feeling they get when they sit down with their families for dinner at night, when they achieve a goal they set, when they find true love—all of it is fake, all of it is not real, and *none* of it lasts forever! We must educate them and, in the process, have *a little feast ourselves*." The two villains laugh with pride and lust for destruction to happen oh-so soon. Then he mutes her with his magic and slams her against the wall, begins choking her, and lifts her ten feet off the stone floor, all of this with not even a wave of his claws. He flashes and appears mere centimeters away from her face, his fire causing her moldy skin to sweat like a pig in a butcher's kitchen.

"Do you swear your blood to my allegiance, to carry out my Jigocrugya, the death to end all life, and to, with every fiber of your existence, consume not just the hope and dreams but the very flesh, blood, organs, and bones of the maleficent Brea family?" Kalypto stops time to wait for her reply. Who is the Brea family and why the hell do they matter so much? That is precisely what Massacara is thinking and tries to voice her opinion but is choking with her weight against his claws. Kalypto can read her mind and is not pleased.

"You damned idiot! Leave that to me however! Should you choose to ignore the Brea family, I will gut you like a fish, feast on your corpse myself, and give your soul a fate so horrid it will pray to be in hell instead." Kalypto's fire has turned red and is roaring so fiercely that chunks of Massacara's face fell off and are sizzling like food in a frying pan. The witch screams in terror and, through her cries, manages to force three words back to him.

"Me…you…forever…" Massacara's spiderweb-like veins grow more and more visible as her life force rushes toward the side of her that Kalypto haunted, and he steals a drop of her oil-like blood from her arm. A single but large explosion of Kalypto's black-and-silver magic erupts like a volcano out of the top of the mountain, and Massacara's crown matches the pattern of Kalypto's horns. From here on out, they are as one. This means that they can detect each other's use of magic, detect each other's presence, and sense any pain in the other. If they are both in the same vicinity, their power will double.

"Yes, my dear, we shall be forever united! To bring this wretched world a taste of its own medicine." He is not happy; he is not cheering or laughing. Instead, he is stone-cold and actually appears entirely filled with rage. His entire life is a lie, and for the last thousand years, he lies in these mountains, stealing their magic and their strength but not enough to kill them and turn them into hilltops; instead, he surgically steals as much proportional magic from them as his father has injected him with a curse. You see, Kalypto has lost any sense of humanity; he lost his conscience when he slaughtered and butchered his father, and he lost his enjoyment from any desire to be good with the murder of his mother. He is an unwanted, hated, and feared orphan who feels the only thing he knew for a fact is that happiness is fake and simply not real. Incapable of being happy, all he felt is rage, vengeance, and hatred.

He is content and thankful for his and Massacara's union and releases her. The jackal moon turns bright green to be as vile as the two adjoined villains. As he storms off, chunks of the Schrie Mountains break apart and fall around them like grim confetti. Individually, their magic is enough to destroy a world, but to combine forces… nothing could stand a chance.

# 8

## Purity and Courage

Meanwhile, after Mage Yidnar has morbidly been forced to witness the murder of his childhood friend being flung from the great balcony at the Palace of the Falls, he too disappears and heads to another friend's location.

Coragio and his wife, Puretia Brea, are of Regulusian descent, meaning they lived in the north not far from the Tree of Fayte. Coragio is not just an ordinary gentleman. He is the captain of the High Archon's guard and an esteemed former member of the Arkanyan military. Remember that Arkanya has disbanded all branches of the military following the celebration of their thousand years of peace. He wears a dark royal-blue tunic with gold buttons and, as a decorated veteran, has medals on his chest. For the Arkanyan military, the custom is to wear medals by order of seniority from left to right, top to bottom, in the shape of an upside-down triangle, the tip of this shape pointing toward the center of the belt buckle. Coragio is a brave man, and young, only in his midthirties. The interesting thing is that despite being a highly awarded officer, he has not yet experienced a single day of combat; Arkanya is celebrating a thousand years of peace after all. He, in his spare time, loves cooking, fishing, and hunting—anything that gets him in the enchanted outdoors. He is a true patriot—loves his country and all the people in it. He married his beautiful strawberry-blonde wife, Puretia, when they were both in their early twenties, having attended the same academy together.

They fell in love upon completing their schooling and started a life together ten years ago. They built their cottage from scratch, but it was high in the trees off the ground, requiring one to take a short flight on the back of an Alicanta, a beautiful, magnificent, large bird of turquoise blue and silver feathers, with an orange beak and black feet. The Alicanta also sings much like the humming of an opera singer. Their house is made of the same wood as the enchanted trees, so as the tree grows, so does their house. By now their house is three stories, and while it is not a luxury resort, it is a charming, warm, and well-loved home.

"Honey, that was a marvelous ceremony today. You and your troops looked so sharp. It's so impressive to see how many people follow you," Puretia says. She kisses her husband and hugs him, welcoming him home.

"Darling, you are the most beautiful in all the land. But thank you! We trained so hard for so long and—" his wife kisses him, and they laugh. He dips his wife like a move from a ballroom dance, something else they love to do.

A few weeks go by and Coragio and Puretia have a routine change. Typically, they will be able to go out after dinner together and experience the beauties of their magical natural world, but tonight is different.

"What shall we do after dinner, rent a boat and watch the stars from the sea? Hike through the woods to the Heatherlyn meadows? I know how much you love those flowers," he suggests. His wife stands up from their table and reveals her belly.

"Honey, I have news for you," she says. They rejoice and dance and are beyond the pale with excitement and joy.

"Well, I guess that means no to boating or hiking!" They laugh again. "Let's stay right here and think about what we'll name our strapping, young boy." Coragio smiles, joining his wife on the couch.

"Our boy?" She smiles and plays coyly, knowing what the truth is, of course.

"Oh, okay, marvelous! What shall we name our sweet baby girl?" he asks. Puretia laughs again.

"Coragio, we've been blessed with three boys." She smiles, but Coragio faints. He is so overjoyed to not have one, not even two, but three! Three little boys, all his sons. Nothing makes him happier, more peaceful, and more stressed thinking about caring for all those babies at once! It is the greatest of blessings to hear but also the most daunting. When Coragio awakes, he is joined by his wife and the family doctor, Argy, and his closest best friend of all, Mage Yidnar. Argy is also a friend from the same academy that Coragio and Puretia attended all those years ago, but the difference is that among the three, Argy went to Acamaro for medical school. Too much distance meant that their friendship turned into messages by bird and occasional enchanted mirror communications, enjoyable but not the same as face-to-face interactions. Argy is tall, slender, and blond. He is athletic and has joined a local sailing club and the Denebian Marine Society, having owned his own yacht. Argy has recently married but does not have children of his own just yet. Rather, they have their own ranch with horses, where he loves to paint landscapes and his wife, Lauretia, enjoys raising the horses and racing them. As a result, he always smells minty fresh from the neck up and about as fresh as a ten-year-old stable from the neck down!

"It's so glorious to see all of you here together. I tell you, I could not be happier if I tried!" Coragio says. Tears of joy trickle down his face as they do down Puretia's, smiling from ear to ear. "To be surrounded by such amazing friends the very day I learn my own little family is growing!" He grabs his friends' shoulders and cheers with their beer steins. Argy rolls his eyes but smiles and laughs with them too. He is a longtime friend and their most trusted doctor of all, but he is more sarcastic and drier than the rest of them!

"Oh, brother, I'm just kidding! Congratulations, you old sack of bones!" exclaims Argy. They laugh again, and smiles are all around and in no short supply.

"Now do tell me what brings you here tonight, Yidnar. I have not seen you in a few months," says Coragio. Yidnar does not want to dampen the high spirits but does seriously need to discuss the prophecy. Most importantly because those three unborn babes might very well be the only thing that can save the future of everyone's world.

"Well, I did have something of the highest urgency to discuss, but we cannot have this talk with Argy around. It's not that we can't trust you. It's that we need to minimize how many ears hear this being explained," Yidnar tries to explain. Argy understands.

"No offense seriously. You three have your talk, and I should be heading home anyway. It's almost the vixen hour. Thanks so much for having me. It was so wonderful to see you lot again! Now remember, Puretia, no physical activity, no heavy lifting, or running. You need rest, and you need to watch your food intake, to mind the foods we discussed are not healthy for you. You are eating for four now!" They all hug and bid him farewell.

Yidnar stands, and his eyes shine bright orange as he places a sensory-dampening spell over the tree house. No one outside the shield can hear them, see them, or otherwise detect them.

"Okay. Right. I always forget you have magic. Anyway, please sit and speak your mind," says Argy.

Yidnar speaks his mind indeed and explains everything, placing on the table the book of records for a few weeks ago when he uncovered and decoded the script of this Propheta Fior. He also explains his loss of his own wife, the death of so many innocent lives in the temple, and the death of the Rex himself.

"My Drakulogon! You can't be serious, Yidnar? Surely it was one of his private soldiers? General Bonmal of the watch of Nauz maybe? Or anyone else who looked like him?" cries Puretia. She cannot believe their ruler has not just died but been murdered by a terrorist witch. They console their dearest friend who has not had any time at all to grieve for the loss of his dearly beloved wife, Liefadra.

"She was everything, my light, my encouragement, my motivation. Now she's gone. Too often I felt I never deserved someone as good and beautiful inside and out as she, but now that I truly lost her, the pain is too much," he cries. Puretia holds his chin up with her fair hand.

"No, Yidnar, you didn't lose her, not entirely. Your love for her will always burn brightly, right there." She gestures at his heart. "You'll never be alone if you remember a part of her will always be with you, with your love for her." They hug, and Coragio drops his glass.

"What is it? What's the matter now?" asks Yidnar.

"I just realized your prophecy essentially predicts the end of the world as we know it, and my wife is about to have children! No matter what witch or demon come this way, we will defeat the monsters. I will not let anything happen to my family, or to you." The stress is mounting ever faster for Coragio.

*****

A few days pass, and the three of them have to process the heavy, dark information Yidnar has just presented them all with. What in the world is their plan? How long do they have to prepare? With the Rex already dead, time is ticking, and no one knows how short they truly have to prepare. As a result, Coragio and Puretia have a private discussion and ultimate agreement to something neither of them like but need.

"You're sure you want to do this? Because while it's a good idea, it also sounds like giving up," cries his wife, her sequined gown sparkling in his arms in the starlight.

"Yes, I am sure. We will fight as hard as we can to protect our family, but if something happens to us, our sons need someone." The two cry. They feel like they are losing their children before they even came into the world. Coragio blows a horn and calls for Yidnar who, with a flash of orange and a rustle of fall leaves, appears in their living room.

"Yidnar, we need to ask you something." Coragio stands and asks.

# 9

## The Creyfather

A rush of anticipation suddenly washes over Yidnar like the waves splashing on the shores of Denebia in the southeast. What can his friend be wanting to ask of him? With all the heavy news dropping of late with the prophecy and what feels like the end of the world, and then the added pressure that only three people not even yet born are the heroes, he is nervous. He has no reason to be though, right?

"Of course, my friend. What's on your mind?" Yidnar asks, taking a sip of mead.

"Well, my wife and I have talked about it, and we feel the time has come to make it official. We want you to be our children's crey-father," Coragio says, both he and his wife smiling so brightly the chandelier feels redundant. Yidnar lets out a huge sigh of relief and then becomes absolutely overjoyed!

"Are you kidding me? Of course, I will! I'll spoil the crap out of them! Anything they want, the answer is yes! As long as it doesn't lead to maim, dismemberment, death, destruction. I am just kidding!" They all laugh at his exaggerations.

"You have been a key figurehead in our little family for many years, and we were trying to think of the best role models for our kids, and no one better than you came to mind," Puretia replies, still smiling widely and gleefully.

"When are the children due?" asks Mage Yidnar. The prophecy is always on his mind He can scarcely think of anything else. Until this time has passed, he will not be able to get a good night's sleep. He is also thinking about the coming funeral for his wife. It is for security for it to be a quiet family-and-close-friends-only event at a local temple out in Denebia for the ocean views and fresh air, both of which Yidnar will need aplenty in order to get through the affair.

"We only found out just a few weeks ago so that would put it at..." All of them connect the dots together simultaneously. Considering it is currently the month of Idajust, a typical nine-month pregnancy would place her due date to be in the week of the middle of Idamay next year. Yidnar teleports to the study where his satchel is with his notebooks and skims through his translated transcriptions of the ethereal message. Orange sparks of magic flew out from Yidnar's hands as he searches for the passage that proclaims the timing of this "event."

Again, the Propheta Fior read, "In the midst of Idamay, there shall be three babes born, each to grow to fight; two unite, each shall bring death and blight, one land to fall with death to all." And so it is confirmed that in the middle of Idamay, just when Puretia is due to give birth, is when the prophecy foretells of a terror to come and bring the end of everything they know and love. Puretia drops her glass as she sobs with worry. Coragio and Yidnar take their seats beside her, consoling her and hugging her.

"Worry not, my love. For if you believe Yidnar about the looming doom, then you must equally and strongly believe him about the light. Our sons are the destined heroes of this land, if we are right. And by the creator, we must have faith that even if it is not our sons, that another trio of heroes will take up the mantle and bring back light to our home. If you believe that, then there is no true threat." The flowers in the room bloom ever fuller just then. The lights all light brighter, and the air smells of flowers to Puretia, the sweetest of chocolates to Yidnar, and of home-cooked meals to Coragio. Someone as pure and as graceful as one can get is approaching.

"My goodness, could it be...?" Yidnar says to himself, completely blown away by what he suspects they are all about to experience and bear witness to. As it happens more often than not, for better or for worse, Yidnar is right. It is the creator of Arkanya, the one true Drakulogon, the Lord of Goodness, the Weaver of Truth, and the Shepherd of Light, Adonai.

Adonai takes the form of a robed male, blond hair at the ends but brunette at the roots, with flowing hair to his shoulders. He is dark-skinned, broad-shouldered, clad in silky, gilded white robes, and has eyes the same shade of blue as Lake Souviens at the basin of the Palace of the Falls. On each finger is a ring from a mineral naturally occurring in each of the five Palacorns; on his head is a Heatherlyn meadow-flower crown and draping over his shoulders is a sash of the limbs from the Tree of Fayte in Regulusio. There is no doubt that this is their god. The one true Drakulogon has graced them all with his presence. Completely taken by surprise and delight and awe, the three friends bow in their god's presence.

"My children, why do you fret so? Do you not trust that in my arms I shall keep safe this land? You and your babes?" says Adonai.

"Father, forgive us our fear. We fret over the thought of being separated from our children, in light of understanding what is to come so soon," replies Coragio. He can't believe he is talking to Adonai; he is beside himself with excitement and intrigue. There is no telling how or why or when this experience happens, and no one believes they'll be blessed enough to be graced with a second and, therefore, wants to make sure to make the absolute most of this meeting.

"My son, the threat you know of is but a freckle upon an apple, a speck of dust upon a great table. It is true that the monsters plan to come to our world, but it is not true to therefore think that all is lost. It may be hard to believe this in the time to come soon. The two monsters who seek to destroy all I have created will indeed come to this world by the middle of Idamay. However, also true is it that your three babes are the ones destined to return light to their darkness. Mark my words, forevermore on the anniversary of the day of their birth, none who wish Arkanya harm shall have any power. That is my gift to you, the only guarantee I can grant without removing free will, which I will never do. There will be more and more times and things that frighten you. But if you let me, I will always be in the stars above to help, for I am the one true Drakulogon, creator of this world, and have given my love to you and to all." Adonai brings the three of them to tears—tears of humility, of an overflowing sense of peace and relief, for who better to protect someone like their children than god himself? He is also profoundly real in his speech, not angry or foreboding, but rather completely understanding and meets them where they are mentally, emotionally, and even spiritually. Adonai truly does love all he has made, but he also truly understands the destruction capabilities of the two prophesied monsters who plan to set things in motion that cannot ever be undone.

"My lord and my Drakulogon, we thank you. We are eternally thankful and appreciative, and we ask only that you continue to grant us peace as you have done and as we strive to live in return," Puretia replies.

"We love you, Drakulogon, Adonai most high, thank you," Yidnar also wants to speak.

"My love goes with all of you. Part now in peace with the knowledge that I too have set things in motion, which cannot be undone. Should you ever be fearful again, simply look up to the stars and remember." With a bright, warm pink and turquoise-and-white flash, Adonai returns from whence he came as easily as he appeared.

# 9

## The Creyfather Part 2

Yidnar thought hard to himself about how to prepare for the future. He went back to his Temple of Prophecies in the northeast and created an elite organization, recruiting the sharpest minds of Arkanya to be his pupils to teach them all he knew about transmuting the most encoded prophecies. He had an intense screening process whereby each applicant would be required to pass a written and practical exam. Applicants were not just accepted from each Palacorn, but they were required. Yidnar needed five people from each Palacorn. He developed with his loving wife a foolproof process whereby he could select the most brilliant minds to not only understand his trade but, should his fearsome new hunch be correct, provide another layer of protection to the most vital pieces to Arkanya's future and existence.

His fear was that the monsters prophesied to bring the greatest destruction and evil to the world would do so in a way that might also harm the heroes—they'd only be babies after all, therefore, less defensive and arguably easier to harm or worse. So seeing as these children were not just children but his creychildren, he wanted to make absolutely certain every base was covered in the worst-case scenario. The stakes were high and felt like they only kept getting higher, this only motivated Yidnar to keep moving, never slumping or slouching, just as his loving wife always knew him to be.

After weeks of recruiting and screening and examining, Yidnar had selected his final troupe of "Praers Guildsmen, I'll call you. Your badge of office will be this bracelet." Yidnar waved his right hand, conjuring on everyone's right arm a copper and marble bracer. "This bracer links us all to one another. It helps us detect where any intended other member is and has the ability to send up a signal to call for aid. Never use this unless you absolutely are outnumbered and near death. This is not 'come help me find my next meal.'" Yidnar was serious about everything as he should be, given the severity of the premonitions. "This is a secret organization ordained by me. Tell only your spouse, no friends, nobody else." Yidnar waved a hand and closed all the doors in the room. "It's time I show you why I am being so serious. What you are about to see is not only what has kept me up at night but also the very near future of this world." Yidnar clapped his hands together and then separated them wide out in front of him, fanning his fingers out and using his orange lit magic to project the full prophecy from the Propheta Fior, illustrating the end of all that was good and wholesome and light in the land. It also showed the death of Yidnar himself and ended with an image of a monster in a nursery with three babies.

"You see, my friends; therefore, I need you. Something wicked this way comes, and it appears we have nothing to defend ourselves, so it is entirely up to us to do everything in our power to conserve, save, and protect the three babies until the end if need be. But, fellow guildsmen, here is where I offer an oath. Swear to me and to Arkanya your loyalty and protection for one another, and most importantly, swear to me if something happens to me, that you'll finish what I started to find the heroes and teach them all I have taught you so that they can fulfill their destiny and bring back the light. Will you swear? You are not obliged to do so. I understand the stakes couldn't be higher, and despite that I am asking each of you to be in between the greatest evil in our existence and the only things destined to stop them, if you leave, I won't blame you. But all would be lost if you do." Yidnar held his head and turned to gaze out the grand window of his temple toward the Palace of the Falls, its magical waterfall gleaming in the sunset twilight. When he turned back around, he smiled and had happy tears of relief, for every member of the guild had stood, raised their right arm, and bowed their heads in his honor. One guildsman in particular was wearing a beautiful emerald-green tunic, high-top brown leather boots, and a strong bow and quiver filled with feathered arrows on his back. The mysterious man had jet-black hair down to his back and a small strand of braids on his left side. He stood and approached Yidnar and knelt at his feet.

"I have loved my country, our country, for all my life, and I would give it to ensure its safety and survival. I swear to you, should it come to it, I will not let anything happen to the prophesied heroes, nor will I sit idly by and let destruction occur. You have my word," replied the guildsman.

"You are noble beyond measure. Is this how you all feel? If not, leave now," Yidnar said. All of the guildsmen and guildswomen knelt and bowed their heads, causing Yidnar to smile victoriously.

"Answer me, all of you! Do you swear never to yield, surrender, retreat, or give up?"

"I do," they replied.

"Will you, if I die, locate, protect, and teach the prophesied heroes all that we know to ensure they fulfill their destiny to save our world?"

"I will," they replied

"And will you rise in unity to defend one another, serve your Rex, Separtino, and banish the evil to the stars?"

"We will!" they all cried out in pride and loyalty.

"Will you defend Arkanya?"

"We will!" They rejoiced and cheered. Yidnar looked down to the gentleman who had approached him earlier and backhanded the man's head with his bracer-clad arm. "Worry you not, my friend. That was so you of all do not forget this." The man smiled and nodded.

"What is your name?" asked Mage Yidnar, with a hand searching for something in his robes.

"My name is Raphael."

"Then, my friends, with the power in me as Chief Divine Seer to the High Archon, I proclaim you all to be Zer, Knights Praer of Arkanya. Despite the cheering and feasting that Yidnar and his followers in the Knights Praer partook, no one else could hear a sound as the celebrations took place beneath the temple, in a secret underground chamber.

"My Lord Yidnar, how might we be able to locate the heroes should something, paradise forbid, happen to you?" asked Raphael.

Yidnar looked at him and stood from the table, halting the celebrations.

"Your fellow knight raises a good question. Should something fatal happen to me when the ultimate day comes, which by the way is the fifteenth of Idamay, precisely ten months from next week, what will any of you do to find the heroes? They could be anywhere in the land, no?" None spoke, they waited for his answers first.

"You will each approach me now and pluck a petal from this Heatherlyn flower. It was the first bud of life other than myself when this world was created. You will all take a petal until the flower replenishes itself and then that person will take possession of the flower. This flower is of the same magical arc as us, to see into the future. Therefore, if you channel your own magic through the petal, you can use it to show you one thing specifically, as a magical map." One by one the knights formed a line and plucked a glowing blue-and-violet petal from the magnificent large old flower, as old as time. There was but one petal left before Raphael had his chance to pluck when suddenly, the flower soared toward the marbled domed ceilings and shined bright as the sun in the room and gently floated down full and lush.

"Very well, Zer Raphael. It belongs to you now. Protect it! Keep it hidden. For the enemy has many eyes, not all of them attached to themselves. We must be trusting of one another and vigilant. Now, eat! And rejoice. you have all done well." A maid came in with wine and drink for the creator of the occasion, and they kissed while everyone cheered and clapped.

# 10

## The Tree of Fayte

### Part 1

Yidnar, Coragio, and Puretia all stammer in a poor attempt to rise to their feet after having just been met by the god of Arkanya, Adonai. It is every bit as amazing as it is unbelievable. No one has seen the Drakulogon since the olden times, centuries upon centuries ago, and he chooses to meet the lot of them. It is truly a blessing, a magnificent encounter, and a moment none of them will ever forget.

"Did that really just happen? Did Drakulogon actually grace us with his presence?" asks Coragio, needing a reality sandwich. He supposes it shan't be so hard to wrap his head around, but it is so incredibly amazing he feels it has to be a dream. That is what makes the whole thing so much better though, isn't it? That Adonai chose to come is not a dream but a real experience all of them are able to share together. Like so many other milestones in their lives, they are there for each other as they have been and always want to remain.

"Yes, my love, it did. And I don't have any fear anymore at all," replies Puretia, crying from her overwhelming experience with Drakulogon.

"He gave you both a gift. Did you catch that? He said that on the day you give birth, anyone who seeks to do harm to Arkanya has no power," replies Mage Yidnar, inscribing this addition to the Propheta Fior as his eyes glow orange.

"Aye, that is true, but if the vile monsters begin before or after, it no longer matters. Nevertheless, that is still an advantage for us. Do you think they know?" asks Coragio.

"I doubt it. Those who have destroyed their hearts to embrace the Yamirzen magic cannot typically even see things from this level of goodness and purity, so no, I believe they do not know." Yidnar hopes he is right, but the only way to know for sure is to wait and hope to survive whenever the monsters do choose to attack.

"Whatever happens, whatever they decide to do, and whenever they decide to do it, I will be here with you, and I will be here for you. I give you my word. I will protect you to the best of my ability. As creyfather to your children, I will protect you with my life," Yidnar pledges to his friends.

"No, Yidnar, that is very sweet and brave, but you mustn't swear to us, for we may not survive, and that may be Adonai's will, or it may not. Fight with us, of course, but instead, please swear to protect my babies. They won't be able to defend themselves," explains Puretia. She appreciates Yidnar with every beat of her heart and is beyond thankful for knowing someone as strong and selfless as he. Yidnar kneels down and holds both of his friends' hands, which glow orange and blue.

"I promise with every breath I take, with every spell I cast, to put your children first, to protect your three sons from any harm in my ability to deflect for as long as I can." There is a flash, and a cloud shaped like a small heart plumes from their hands. The three friends hug, and Puretia cries with both gratitude and love.

"I must leave you now. There are some things I must attend to in order to prepare for the coming of these monsters. Please take these, three for each of you. Simply shout my name and smash these crystals on your chest over your heart, and no matter where I am, I will teleport to you. Protect these for when they are depleted, that's it," Yidnar explains. The crystals are called Pertez, a glowing, magical, crystal orb about the size of an orange, which serve ever only one purpose determined by their creator wizard. In this case, they are summoning crystals intended to bring forth Mage Yidnar shall things get bad on the hour of the birth of the heroes, but they can be created to serve any purpose so long as it is one purpose and causes no harm nor facilitates destruction, breaks the three laws of magic, and so forth.

"Thank you, my friend. I hope we don't need to use these, but we certainly will if the moment comes. We'll notify you by bird once my wife goes into labor and she delivers our prophesied sons," Coragio states. He holds his wife close, and they hug their friend goodbye for now.

Yidnar turns on his heel, and as he walks away waving farewell, a whirling rustle of leaves trickles and gently floats down to the ground where he walked moments before. Like he said, he has things to do and less and less time to do them in.

First on his list is to practice using magical items like wands and staves. He normally is strong enough to not need either but is also anticipating a great battle against formidable, foul foes when "it" begins. He travels to the northwest region of Regulusio to visit the Tree of Fayte. Luckily for Yidnar, the journey is cut by a third, as he is beginning his journey from Coragio and Puretia's home instead of his own. Even still, it will be a twelve-week journey one way due to the fact that whenever one visits the Tree of Fayte, one must only travel on foot, the old-fashioned way, as Yidnar refers to it. He decides to follow the River Eirini from the Souviens Lake as that will not only provide him with thirst quenching water but also magical nourishment.

He strides along for days on end, being magically energized by the Eirini waters but eventually, after a week, needs to rest. He motions with his hands and leaves from trees begin weaving together into sheets for the top of a tent; a tree stump becomes chopped into small logs and ignited for a campfire, and he opens some of the containers of food his late wife has packed for him, and he prepares his dinner under the stars.

"Liefadra, how I love you. Thank you, Adonai, for all that you do in my life and everyone else's," Yidnar says a thoughtful prayer before his meal and thinks about the wonderful times he shared with his wife. Suddenly, he remembers he is near Lake Souviens. He gazes up at the stars, and the moon is full. The moon is still a jackal moon (face of a skull), but it is full. *Maybe*, he thinks to himself that it is worth a try. He steps into the lake and rolls up his pants and robes past his knee and creeps into the river, feeling the scales of fish and plants brush against him.

He closes his eyes and hopes strongly for the visage of his wife to appear, despite his not being in the lake.

"I hear your call, my love. While I cannot appear to you, I can speak with you for a brief moment. What is on your mind?" The echoing voice from beyond belongs to his dearly beloved wife.

"My darling, I miss you so much. I have no purpose other than to talk with you. I miss the conversations and holding you in my arms. I'll need you with me more than ever before. There is an evil coming, an evil we have not faced before."

"Actually, Yidnar, that is not true. Not only has Arkanya faced one of them before, but you have also now faced both. The witch who took my life and the horned specter who waged war a thousand years ago—it is them," echoes the helpful ghostly voice of his lost wife. Even after death she is helping him. Yidnar grows an immense desire to annihilate the two cretins to avenge his wife and preserve Arkanya. "I can see I just set you off on a heroic quest. Just make sure you remember your promise to Coragio and Puretia. You promised to protect their children. Please don't let my death steer you away from that because no matter how hard you kill them, if you do, I can't come back. That's all part of life though, isn't it? Death is not an ending, my love. Tonight is proof." She, of course, cannot be seen, but Yidnar knows in his heart she is not only right but smiling.

# 11

## The Tree of Fayte

### Part 2

The next morning, Yidnar places a reversal spell on the campsite, returning the firewood logs to the tree stump, unweaving the tent, placing the leaves back on the tree, and extinguishing and vanishing the fire. He eats some additional food from his pack and washes his face with water from the Eirini River, fondly remembering the night before, having one last conversation with his late wife. As he hikes through the trees, he admires the beauty and the peace of Arkanya, though it feels out of place. Terrible things have already begun to happen, starting with the death of his wife, leading to the attack on the temple during the coronation, and finally with the murder of the High Archon, the Rex of Arkanya himself.

With the man at the top gone, only the eldest of the High Princeps—the leaders of each Palacorn—is eligible to take the mantle until a vote in the council can be made for deciding the next ruler. That vote must wait eight months until it can go into session. Until then, the High Princep who leads in the Rex's place must finish the former leader's plans that have already been started. Any plans that have not yet begun the process from approval to fruition are to be disregarded. As such, the High Princep is quite busy with the heavy administrative focus in the first few months of taking office. After that is completed, the next phase is the High Princep can implement any two new plans he or she so desires as long as it aligns with the Great Concorde—the incredibly lengthy document detailing the dos and don'ts of all government officials and operations. After that is completed, the Council of Princeps (all other Princeps who do not take the Rex/Rexa's place) will hold a vote to decide of all the officials in Arkanya who is best suited to be the next High Archon.

Back and forth. Mystagio paces along the halls, never getting anything done, just toiling over page upon page of silly useless words, angering the people of Arkanya.

"Why is nothing being done after the Rex himself was murdered by a magicked terrorist?"

"How do we save our children?"

"Where were the armed guards when our families were slaughtered?" The crowds grow in number and in anger. The mob of angry citizens has amassed and is fed up. Fed up with nothing being done for seven months. Fed up with the people they love being made to feel like waste to be gotten rid of as carelessly as hazardous materials. Fed up with how much time the powers that be wasted thinking about everything the former Rex wanted to complete before he was cut down before his prime. The shouts, cries, yells, and uproar are so loud one could scarcely hear anything else.

Suddenly, there is a loud bang as the High Princep Mystagio conjures a judge's mallet and rams it down on the crumbling and destroyed Balcony of Defeat as he uses magic to levitate and project his voice.

"People of Arkanya, please keep order! QUIET!" he roars, his voice echoing throughout the land. "Good, thank you. Now, as you know, this is all just part of our process. I think the bigger issue at play here is the fact that with a thousand years of peace we've forgotten how to operate and mitigate certain circumstances in times of duress. As such, it is important to remember that we developed this system as a form of governmental accountability to allow administrative staff the time to address the issue of losing the ruler and time to allow the public, you all, to ponder who you'd like to succeed the great Rex Separtino. It is also important to remember that there are no actions we can take yet to mitigate the threat of this magnitude.

What I am here to announce to you all today is that the Arkanyal Corps of SOLS has been fully reactivated, and we are recruiting members today. If you meet the specified requirements for becoming a SOLS, a delivery of information will magically arrive at your current place of residence. All others who do not qualify, feel free to apply to our medical corps of surgeons, doctors, and nurses. Any others, please carry on your glorious lives in peace and please stay calm. Until the time that our SOLS are ready to defend Arkanya, I will personally place a protection shield over the country at precisely the time when the jackal moon soars above the trees this evening. It will be imperative to converse with the Tree of Fayte for your pilgrimage prior to this event, as the shield may interfere or completely inhibit the tree's ability to respond verbally. Thank you!" The people of Arkanya are silent, taking in the information. On the one hand, they are pleased the SOLS (Special Forces of Ocean Land and Sky) are active duty again but are at the same time scared that the looming threat is deemed so legitimate that they've rebuilt the strongest forces from the former military. The crowd then erupts into applause for their approval. No cheers, no celebratory exclamations, just applause. Afterward, the people of Arkanya return to their homes, but instead of preparing dinners and enjoying time by the fire with their families, they teach their children how to fight, in case there comes a time soon when that will be needed.

As Yidnar hikes onward, now only a few weeks away from the Tree of Fayte, he lets out a loud strangely high-pitched yawn, which is so out of the ordinary he laughs at himself a bit. As he looks around, he sees how much things have changed. Gazing at homes in the distance, he sees people being fitted for uniforms and armor, target practice in backyards, and other various tactical forms of engagement.

*This is good but also sad*, he thinks to himself. Like the rest of Arkanya, Yidnar wants only what is best, and sadly, right now that means the end of peacetime activities. The motivation, however, is to ensure there will be a country for peacetimes to be had in the future, for the level of threat that the prophecy revealed is one of the highest orders ever experienced. As the sun sets, he remembers what the High Princep announced this morning regarding the communication with trees being limited or completely impossible verbally. He moans with annoyance. This will make things unorthodox but not difficult for him.

Suddenly, as he continues walking and drinking water he grabbed from the Eirini River, he sees it: Standing bright with magic and tall and proud is the magnificent tree to end all trees, its trunk as wide as a palace and the crown of the tree far above the clouds. Each twisting and bark-covered branch bent in some new, curvy way; every carriage-sized leaf is a varying shade of green, blue, yellow, and red, draping down over the country like a canopy.

The tree can visibly be seen inhaling and exhaling slowly and deeply. Fayte is very much alive with both nature and magic, as alive as every person in Arkanya. It is taught in schools throughout Arkanya correctly that this tree is the very first living thing in Arkanya. The tree, hugs at the roots by the Heatherlyn meadow, long ago has nestled in the northwestern region of Regulusio, and a fraction of her roots drape into the banks of the Eirini River directly connecting Lake Souviens and, by extension, every branch of the Eirini River and every Palacorn of Arkanya. In many ways, both literal and figurative, the Tree of Fayte is the heart of Arkanya.

Yidnar reaches the roots of the tree at last, which are as gargantuan as sea mammals and as long as the river. Indeed, the roots of Fayte stretch far and wide across all regions of the country, deep underneath the ground.

A few weeks later, Yidnar approaches the tree and sits down to rest after such an arduous hike across the region.

Finally, after washing his face, he holds one of the low hanging branches of leaves and begins the "meeting." High Princep Mystagio is correct that verbal communication is so hindered. All Yidnar can hear is in his head, not from an external source. The tree is speaking to him telepathically. But a soft hum can Yidnar hear as the connection stabilizes and strengthens between them.

"Yidnar, at last you return. How good to once again uproot your path," the tree speaks.

"Fayte, you are always a sight for sore eyes. I would love to divulge poems for you as we have done before, but alas, my meeting with you is of a far more serious nature."

"Go on." The tree, though pure and good and indeed powerful and alive, is not omnipotent.

Yidnar reveals and explains the Propheta Fior, how it correlates with his friends' unborn children, and the two monsters who have yet to bring their true attack on the world. He starts to explain what the government is doing to prepare, but the tree cuts him off.

"I understand. What is it you seek with me?" asks the tree.

"I may need a branch or two. If the witch and the specter bring what I think they can, I'm going to need every fail-safe possible."

"Yidnar, for the protection of your people and perhaps yourself, I grant you the ability to sever a branch at your whim to use as you wish, so long as it aligns with my purity. Otherwise, it will disintegrate. Help will always come to those in Arkanya, to those who ask for it, and are pure of intentions. For it is not an action alone that generates or dictates what is evil or good, but also intention. Killing another with magic at first sounds terrible, but if it saved the lives of thousands more would that not be a good thing?" asks the tree.

"Lives are all important and to be cherished, not to be rationalized away with grade school math," Yidnar replies, thinking about his wife and the innocents lost in the temple.

"Perfect answer. My gift is confirmed, and your time is up. Farewell, Master Yidnar. Until Idamay." And the tree falls back to sleep, her leaves gently billowing in the evening summer breeze. The sun is setting on the end of the eighth month and final full day before the next Rex/Rexa is to be elected, and Puretia is to birth the heroes.

# 12

# Birth

After his encounter with the Tree of Fayte, a pilgrimage many faithful Creytians strive to take in their lifetime, Yidnar teleports back to his home away from home, the Temple of Prophecies, though nowadays it feels more of a graveyard or war zone than a cherished sacred temple. Yidnar uses magic to bury each body in an organized, charming, and respectful graveyard near the back courtyard and sends out magical owls to deliver news of this new site to the good people of Arkanya who have lost someone on that fateful evening.

That settled, he lively steps into his private enchanted study where within its walls he transcribes a very particular set of premonitions and prophecies—those regarding his own future. He can only fully translate one of them, and the very moment he finishes translating and recording the message in his Book of the Undone, there is a terrible flash of orange light and a soft voice speaking to him.

"Mage Yidnar, you have attempted to peek into your own future, and so you have jeopardized your Crey-given gift of free will. Do you wish to know that which you sought? If not, the prophecy stone shall crumble, and all will be as it should. If you do, the future will be uncertain, and the might of the heroes destined to return light to Arkanya will be hindered," speaks the familiar and friendly feminine voice from beyond.

"Liefadra, is it you who came to warn me of my transgressions? My love, even after death you aid me and guide me," Yidnar attempts to hold the ethereal woman's face affectionately until he hears a laughter so maniacal and so painful his ears bled, and he screams in agony. He can feel Yamirzen magic holding his heart to make it difficult to beat. The figure from his desk hovering above his own prophecy stone smothers away, and in a magenta flash, there appears none other than Massacara, who comes to deliver her precise torture.

"You wastrel fool! 'Liefadra, Liefadra, I love you.' SHEATHE YOUR TOXIC TONGUE!" Massacara uses such powerful magic she can now control Yidnar from wherever the oblivion she is at the time. Her dagger-clad hands pins Yidnar to his own wall, and the grip on his heart grows tighter like a boa constrictor's death squeeze.

"Release me, witch! You'll regret the day you were born!" Suddenly, the witch tightens her grip as hard as she can, very nearly killing Yidnar as he lets out louder screams than he has ever before. The hellfire image of Massacara's hideousness and cruelty grows larger and closer to him against the wall until he can feel the heat from her dark, forbidden, toxic magic.

"You have nothing. No future, no wife, no children, no legacy. Everything you've ever wanted, I have eaten! Do you want to know how juicy dreams are? Imagine the ripest of oranges, one bite on that tender and raw bit of meat you call hope, and everything crumbles. You know it's almost better than sin! I digress, anyway, I have eaten anything that can motivate you, and anything that can strengthen you to give me a real threat. What you just said was empty. You think I don't hate the day I was born? I'll show you *real* pain and sadness, my little hero! There'll be more heat in your heart tomorrow than any other day of your *life*!" The witch cackles and laughs in concert with cursed split echoes of her wretched voice, leaving Yidnar who barely has enough energy to cry, scream, or fight back. He thinks to himself just how wrong Massacara is. The love he shared with his late wife can never be defeated, not by her or anything else. He is not okay to be cut down before he can fulfill his best friend's promise, however. With every magical ounce of blood in his veins, he gathers all the magic to his eyes and channels his magic to teleport away, just before it is too late.

"Curses! You coward! No matter, my little soldier, take all the time you need, for tomorrow we fight not just to defeat each other but for your home and everyone you love." Massacara's words hang in the air like a lingering fire, which burns to a crisp every living plant in the vicinity. The grass withers away and dies, leaving behind a thick, muddy ash; neighboring trees moan as they crack their trunks and topple over, changing the beautiful, magnificent forest to a spike-filled ocean of spears. Whatever spell Massacara has up her sleeve, one thing became clear: it is not the end of the world she has planned.

Still recovering from the snake-like grip on his chest, Yidnar returns to the Tree of Fayte, guessing that the witch cannot detect his magic there. He is furious. He wants to protect the beautiful land he lives in so much but only has one idea. It is one idea sure, but so far, his guess seems to be correct, that the witch cannot detect him shall he be right next to the Tree of Fayte.

Suddenly, Mage Yidnar feels a tingling in his chest, and just as quickly as it arrives, it left. Again, he feels a shudder from his heart to his feet, which reminds him of the parting gift he bestowed to his friends, the Brea family: the Pertez crystals, magical crystal orbs filled with water from the Souviens Lake and laced with teleportation properties from charms found in the dust of crushed runes in the South Mountains. Together they magically adhere and form a beautiful marbly material glowing multiple shades of blue, green, and pink.

Yidnar looks up, remembering what the witch said about his own prophecy, that he has no future. Is this truth, or is it lies meant to derail his strength? He swallows a bit of fear and answers the call, returning to his friends in a whoosh of rustling autumn glowing leaves. He cannot help but notice the effect Massacara has on his heart. His very chest is blackened like someone spilled dark ink all over his chest, and it feels sharp to the touch.

He arrives at quite a chaotic scene: nurses and Doctor Argy all dressed in the purest white, rushing from room to room, gathering the tools and things they need to help in the birth of the oh-so important three babes.

Yidnar remembers that today is the fifteenth of Idamay, the very day the Propheta Fior declared the monsters will bring upon Arkanya the greatest evil their world has ever experienced and the day that the only people who can stop it are born. There is no way to magically ID the babies. There is only for Yidnar to gamble that these children are in fact the ones aforementioned and to have hope that he is correct.

"Yidnar, my brother, you came. We were so hopeful you'd make it!" Coragio hugs his dear friend as tears of the most peaceful joy roll down his strong cheeks.

"I couldn't miss the birth of my creysons now, could I?" Yidnar returns the admiration and affection. Puretia yells as she labors through the contractions to prepare to push the first hero, their first son to the world.

Dr. Argy comes running over as Puretia yells more frequently, telling him this is it.

"Come on, Puretia, push! Push! You can do it," he encourages Puretia who, despite sweating and frowning with the birth pains, is also deliriously happy. This is the one moment she has prayed for, to grow her family. She looks up at her beloved husband with her shimmering, radiant reddish-blond hair and tries to smile but almost comedically can't as she yells once more. Coragio holds her and grabs her hand tightly.

"Remember your breathing darling," he imitates the pattern Dr. Argy informed them she needs to maintain. She holds his hand tighter and tighter, fighting through the pain but no longer yelling.

Dr. Argy smiles so wide it looked as if he is staring at a pot of gold. Indeed, he is looking at something far more precious.

"Your firstborn son! Coragio! Puretia! Your first son is here! He's a beautiful, healthy baby boy, blue-eyed like his father." They all laugh and smile and sniff through the tears. It is truly a magical moment as the baby's eyes shine bright blue, and up on the ceiling, an ethereal glittering waterfall fell down and slowly turns to magical snow, each flake the same beautiful aqua blue but different in its artistic design. Puretia holds out a hand and catches two of the magical snowflakes, which begins to gleefully hug each other and dance in her palm, the way she dances with her husband. Yidnar can't believe the immense sense of joy he feels holding the littlest babe in his arms after Dr. Argy and Coragio clean him up. The joy is much like the magical waterfall the baby conjured, washing over them and bringing naked and deep bliss. Yidnar hands the baby boy with glowing blue eyes, as sapphire gems harkening to the deep blue oceans, to his mother.

"Ayton Brea, you are the sweetest boy in all the land." She smiles and kisses his little nose. Ayton grabs her ear with his tiny hand and smiles. Yidnar waves a glowing orange hand and summons a beautiful rosewood crib big enough and safe enough for the three of them and holds Ayton in his arms.

"I'm your creyfather, Ayton, how nice to meet you." They both smile widely, and Yidnar's heart can't feel more at peace. Dr. Argy runs right back over to the end of the table she lies on, near her legs, to prepare for the second child.

"Okay, next one, Puretia. I need you to push for me, come on puuush!" Dr. Argy eggs her on, eager and excited to meet the next Brea family member.

Again, she squeezes and squeezes Coragio's hand as hard as she can, replicating the breathing again but this time the pain is greater. She let out a symphonic yell as the head of her second son emerges. Dr. Argy takes him and cleans him up and Coragio names him this time, holding the smiling sweet, beautiful baby boy in his arms close to him for warmth.

"Baelac Brea, you are the strongest young boy in all the land. Your father loves you, your mother loves you, and look! Your creyfather is here for you too!" The father and his second son embrace and smile so much their cheeks hurt. The little babe has the most enchanting, glowing emerald eyes as green and charming as the enchanted forests. Just then, all the flowers and plants in the room grow larger and more vibrant. A little moon flower jumps out of its pot, bows to the family, and becomes a beautiful family brooch. The mother has a beautiful enchanted Heatherlyn flower crown, and the father has a sash of willow leaves as the flowers in the room cheer and clap and nourish the mother to not feel pain with childbirth. All of them gaze in awe and amazement as the fields surrounding their house in the trees conjure the most fruitful and plentiful farms imaginable. Enough crops and food for eons to come.

"Baelac, you are so loved for all time," says the mother as she kisses Baelac's forehead, and Yidnar holds him. Those gorgeous emerald eyes are staring back at him as if to form a response! But surely babies as young as these can do no such thing. For the third and final time, Dr. Argy comes to the foot of the bed for aid in delivering the third and final brother to the triplets.

"You know the drill, Puretia, push! Come on, sweetie, you can do it. Puuush!" And with cries, the third and final prophetical son is delivered. Dr. Argy carries the newborn babe over to be cleaned with the nurses, and Yidnar gazes in amazement as the ceiling portrays the most incredible starry sky anyone has ever seen—meteor showers, galaxies, constellations, and other stars and systems shine brilliantly upon the domed ceilings. Everyone watches in amazement as the third babe with beautiful bright-red eyes like rubies from the South Mountains. It is not an abrasive deep red like fire or danger, but rather a magnificent, confident bright red.

"Dantiel Brea, you are loved by everyone in this room. You are strong and cherished, my sweet boy." Puretia kisses him the same way she did her other two sons, and the three magical children light up the room with their blue, green, and red eyes.

"Puretia, our family is here." Coragio holds his beautiful babies with Yidnar's help, and the six wonderful people cherish the moment together as sacred as the time they were met by Adonai himself. For this is the beginning, the true legacy anyone can lay bare—children. Pure of heart, full of strength, and the heirs of the family. Everyone stands still, loving each other in so much harmony you could almost hear music. All three of the boys clearly are born with the magika blood cell, with each of their gifts to their parents the moment they are born, almost as if they said thank you through their magical delivery.

"In all my years as a doctor, I have delivered countless children, but none of them ever showed power like that. You truly are blessed by Adonai. I can see it and feel it." The doctor turns on his heel to continue cleaning and packing up everything, just when a harsh, pink light fills the room.

"My boys, hear me and remember it for as long as you live. Be brave, have strength, and love always." Puretia kisses them on their foreheads as the babies cough, and white sparkling dust sprinkles from the kiss to their hearts with her blessing.

"What is that?" asks Puretia.

Yidnar immediately casts as much magic as he can.

"EVERYONE, GET DOWN. THE WITCH IS COMING!" He runs around the house with both of his magical hands firing spells left and right. The pink light grew hotter and brighter as the witch reaches closer and closer, the seconds slipping away faster and faster.

"Dr. Argy, you must leave at once!" Yidnar says, trying as hard as he can to lock and seal every door, window, or crevasse he can find while again lacing them all with magic dampening spells to hinder the entrance of the vile witch. He arrives back in the grand foyer and uses magic to teleport the nurses away to their respective homes, casts spells to create a force field around the children in their cribs, sending them away from their loving parents' arms and engulfed by magical orange egg-shaped shields. Yidnar also conjures an ethereal sword as twisted and serrated as he can muster. Coragio draws his sword from his dusty sheath and holds his wife tightly close to him She cannot be moved so soon after childbirth. The heat and light coming from Massacara is so great all of them are sweating profusely and feeling weaker due to dehydration. Yidnar casts another charm to protect the children, but in his efforts, neglects Coragio, Puretia, and Dr. Argy. The priority is the children; it has to be the children. Nothing can derail that purpose. The fates and lives of everyone in the world depend on it.

"Everyone in position. We have no time to lose! She's here!" orders Yidnar, placing protection spells on everything from the tree branches supporting the house to the rooms the children are in. The entire house hums with his magical energy as everyone holds tight and braces for the evilest impact. He rushes Coragio and Puretia near the hospital bed and the children into their planned nursery. He pulls from out of his sleeve a tree branch he had taken from his last meeting with the Tree of Fayte. *I wonder*, he thinks to himself, his brain hatching an idea to make magic from magic rather than make magic, by channeling his own using the blessed tree's magic instead. He uses magic with the Tree of Fayte's branch and places a cloaking spell over the three of them to be and remain for now unseen by the witch. Just then, a great, flaming pink ball of fire and smoke crashes through the house, destroying the roof, walls, and windows and obliterating Yidnar's protection force field. All over the floor is the signature thick, black muck, and it boils piling atop itself, slowly forming into the revolting witch known as Massacara, standing just at the end of the room. She lets out a victorious cackle, causing the babies to scream and the parents to have their ears bleeding.

"Enchanting, my friend. How's your wife?" Massacara is so proud of her murdering his wife she almost looks happy. Almost instantly, Massacara transforms into a slenderer version of herself, except that dress with the spike-covered pleats morphed into tar-dripping tentacles, and she slithers along the floor casting pink-colored killing curses left and right, attempting as hard as she tries to murder the Brea parents. Coragio's sword has been blessed by a priest in Leonulia with celestial magic and, as a result, has the ability to block spells. The blade glows bright pink as it absorbs the curses and expels them back at their caster. It is unknown to the witch where the children are.

Pink and orange magic burst and explode in the room, humming as it flew through the air to its intended victim. Yidnar becomes blooded by the umpteenth spell cast at him, and Massacara shows an inhuman ability to keep going. Yidnar is getting tired and needs both to rest as well as recharge his magic. Using his magic this long is the equivalent of running a marathon, sweating, panting, and heart racing. Every fiber of his being is involved in protecting the friends he loves. Their fighting has focused on just each other, and they have drifted to the patio on the outside of the house elevated high in the trees, away from the Brea parents and the children. Suddenly, there is a terrible gut-wrenching scream from a woman. Massacara is not Massacara at all and waves goodbye at Yidnar as the illusion ended. Yidnar has been essentially fighting smoke this entire time, with the real Massacara inside the house torturing Puretia and Coragio. Yidnar's heart sinks. How can he has not seen through her trickery? No time to despair, he runs back inside and uses both hands to fire magic at her, the bolts of magic exploding like mini orange bombs, damaging the house and indeed bringing the wretched witch pain.

"Too late. You failed," Massacara hisses.

"No! How is this...how can... I was just... No!" Yidnar roars. He is confused; he does not understand how his friends can already be dead. The fight with the fake witch must have gone on longer than he anticipated. Yidnar runs over to the place his best friends are lying blooded and gasping for breath. They both have tears rolling down their faces and try desperately to talk to him.

"You...didn't have to..." Coragio attempts to say that Yidnar doesn't have to come back for them. He knows what happened, and it is too late, but he doesn't hold Yidnar accountable. He cries so hard, missing his children already and his best friend, for he knows he is entering a place Yidnar will not follow, and he hopes, for a long time. Coughing up more blood, Massacara can be seen in the background literally destroying the house, searching for the children, screaming for the answer to where they are. Yidnar cries hard, feeling guilty, and agreeing with the witch that he failed them.

"You were...trying to prot..." Puretia cries and bleeds out more, trying to tell him she knows he is just trying to protect them, that she understands he has been deceived. Yidnar lies on the floor with his dying best friends, and his eyes sting from the sweat and tears pouring down his cheeks. He tells his friends he loves them.

"I will protect your children if it is the last thing I do," Yidnar swears now. He stands, rising up to find Massacara has damn near destroyed the entire house, ripping it apart plank by plank to find the children.

"You won't find them. I have used skills beyond your comprehension, you simpleminded freak. So why don't you do us all a favor and go jump off your own cliff! Or did you need some assistance with that?" Yidnar yells at the evil witch. She cackles again, causing his ears to bleed further.

"You couldn't even beat my fake self. Now you want to fight me? No, you're not ready. Once you can destroy an entire population, then come talk to me. Until then?" She snaps her dagger-clad arms and appears so close to him he is smashed against the wall.

"Leave me alone and rest assured, my brave little hero, that I will find those three beasts, and I will skin them before feasting in the greatest frenzy of all time on their delicious souls."

"I'll be ready whenever you're brave enough to face me, coward!" Yidnar strikes a magical blow at the entire section of the house above Massacara and sends it cascading down upon her, but in the last second, she teleports away.

Yidnar whispers to himself, "It worked!" Yidnar is relieved. He is relieved he has a weapon the villain can't detect but knows he has very little time and also still remorseful of the loss of his dear friends. He uses his magic to privately and safely bury them, giving them gilded headstones. He uses the Wand of Fayte again to reveal the children and holds them together tightly in his arms, their beautiful, powerful eyes glowing smartly under the fire-red sunset.

"Stay strong, you three. You need to come with me now." He scoops them up in his arms and suddenly, the second born son, Baelac Brea, uses magic again to conjure a beautiful wreath of roses around the stones and plants beautiful cherry blossom trees, looking like peace is snowing to the ground where they lay. Yidnar kisses Baelac's forehead in amazement and thanks and says to him, "You lot are going to be the most powerful wizards in any world." And they vanish.

# 13

## Fire and Death

Yidnar appears in a clap of thunder and swirl of autumn leaves, glowing his signature orange hue. They appear at the banks of the Souviens Lake nearing the middle of the night. It is a bittersweet moment for sure. While Yidnar loves his three creysons, he weeps for the loss of their parents, his dearest friends. The children are by no means newborn babes at this point. It is mysterious as it is a blessing. While only moments have passed since the fateful attack on the Brea parents, the children appear to be between the ages of two and four.

Yidnar has only just noticed, as he is preparing to set up a force field. "What the?" He laughs as he sees the children now have teeth and hair, and despite being triplets, all look unique. Baelac has curly, blond hair, as curly as pasta and as golden as sunshine His skin is fair, and his hands are large. Ayton has brown, straight hair as thick as rope and as brown as chocolate. He is tan, has enormous feet, and broad shoulders. Lastly, there is Dantiel who has black hair like the mane of a horse. He too is tan, possibly the tannest of the three and definitely the tallest. Ayton can scarcely keep his balance, to which Yidnar laughs and laughs as he helps teach him how to walk and talk.

"I should never have had to do this, but I wouldn't trade these moments for anything in the world, and I will love you three forever," he says. Just then, the archmagi of the Temple of Prophecies, Mage Yidnar, hears a collection of noises he really is in no mood to hear—screams of death.

In the far distance, Yidnar uses his elf-like vision to see hundreds of miles away as some dark army travels to his direction, with nothing but pure fire in its wake. It begins to rain not water but fire! Fire that is burning, disgusting, stinking black muck. Yidnar grows tired of his location and intentions being spied upon, so he grabs the Wand of Fayte from his sleeve and says to himself, "I have no patience for small wands. A staff you are now," and punches the air downward while firmly holding the wand, which glows orange and grows to be as long as he is tall, and the crown of the staff is a beautiful wooden twirling of branches inside which is a magical ember providing light far ahead. He uses the Staff of Fayte to conjure a shield to protect them from the hellfire raining down upon them. "RUN!" Yidnar yells. The kids follow suit and, enhanced by Yidnar's magic, run as fast as they can back to the Tree of Fayte, as far away as possible from the mysterious fire. In the distance too, Yidnar can make out red flares shooting up into the sky, the harrowing sight of members of his guild, the Knights Praer, being outnumbered and outmatched, and killed by the Skrall Army, their disgusting forms dripping with black muck, their arms as swords and worms or cockroaches for teeth in their rotting skulls. The good people and the Knights of Arkanya are all slowly defeated.

*****

An hour ago, Massacara has returned to reunite with Kalypto and provide an update on her progress. The ground beneath her becomes covered in a bewitching black ice; everything living grows dark and unable to move or speak or do anything but feel pain.

"Lord of Malice, the Purity and the Courage of Brea have fallen," speaks Massacara, her tentacular gown still flailing about like an apocryphal octopus. Kalypto reveals himself as a white misty haze with menacing silver claws the size of a shrub and with nails as sharp as the horns on his skull.

"You have failed, you filthy slave. Your orders were to cut the children down as infants, and you couldn't even do that. What a miserable creature you are. Tell me, did your father approve of your inability to accomplish even the most retarded of tasks? I'd wager not as I contemplate your usefulness to me." With every inch that he approaches Massacara, she weeps and hates herself almost as much as Kalypto hates himself. He uses his dark Yamirzen magic to hold Massacara up off the ground by her hair, what little of it she has left, and she screams in agony. "All you will ever feel so long as you remain stupid is pain, am I clear? Your task grows now. I strike away your task to kill only the Brea children. You must now KILL ALL LIVING THINGS IN THIS WORLD! EVERY MAN, WOMAN, CHILD, ANIMAL, DOWN TO THE LAST MICROBE SHALL BE EXTERMINATED! I ORDER THE EXTINCTION OF ARKANYA! Is that clear? Kill all, or die," Kalypto yells deeply. With every roar of his rage, the mountain trembles, struggling to contain his wrath and wickedness. He wants everything dead—vegetation, habitations, everything.

"My lord, there is no such spell in Yamirzen strong enough to accomplish that," she says. Massacara again shrieks with piercing pain as Kalypto tears chunks of her flesh off, eating it like a snack.

"I thought we went over this. Either kill everything or be killed. It's that simple and should you—" This time, it is he that is interrupted. Massacara casts a spell at him, firing a bolt of her pink energy as hard as she can, sending him blasted back against the mountainside.

"I am not a fool, you wretched being. There are no spells that can accomplish what you wish. I have learned every spell and piece of black magic in the Book of Yamirzen. It does not exist. So if you wish to do this, find your own way. I'm out." Massacara suddenly begins to be stuck in her place, and the amethyst crown breaks off her skull and falls to the floor, dimming and disintegrating. The reign of the witch is over. Kalypto has cleaved his enormous claws deep inside her chest, tearing away her soul from her body, ripping her in two. With the death of the evilest witch in creation, there is an enormous magical explosion, and Kalypto moans as his own power grows, his misty form filling with pink, black, and red magic from her dying body.

"Your stupidity and sense of self blinded you from the true meaning of power within Yamirzen." Kalypto steals Massacara's magic from her soul, taking every drop of her blackened magika blood as his own and boosting his power tenfold.

The fire in his skull illuminates ruby red and viciously roars through his jaw and empty eye sockets.

"Let's begin." He chuckles. At Massacara's dead body, there lays a black satchel within which is the stone to summon the Shi Army. He breaks her arm backward, ripping the satchel off her deceased body. He also plucks out the heart of Massacara, for in order to cast what he calls the Jigocrugya, you need to have the heart of the greatest deceiver and the blood of the cruelest demon. Now that he has both, he crushes the heart to make a liquid, stirring the concoction with her own bones.

He merely looks at the potion, and it overflows, filling the mountain to the brim and bursting with explosive power like a volcano of magical, cursed death. Kalypto floats a specter through the mountain to the very top to watch the end of all things good.

The hellfire brings clouds with it and rains down upon first the southwest region of Arkanya, setting ablaze the lush farms, killing the food, the citizens, bathing them in flaming tar, stopping them dead in their tracks wherever they are—huddled together as a united, loving family, shielding a loved one from the dangers, or otherwise trying to stave off the doom alone. None escapes its death grip as the Jigocrugya erupts from the South Mountains and endlessly spews molten lava glowing ruby red all over.

The trees scream as they shrivel up in the fires and burn to a crisp; the animals turn to stone and become feral, ferocious beasts with diseases and a thirst for blood, helping the death spread. The flowers that once are charming and helpful turn into traps as large as a house but as hidden as a mouse and can digest a man in seconds. The rivers glow green with toxicity, and the birds breathe more fires like that from the Jigocrugya, like miniature dragons. Everything good and beautiful has wilted and died and, in the ashes of the corpses of the charred Arkanyans, is reborn into the blackest of nightmares.

# 14

## aynakrA

As the Jigocrugya rains down upon the innocent lives of Arkanya, the death of not just the people but the beautiful magic that is its nature can also be heard dying—the screams of the people, the shrieks of the trees, and the roars of the animals as the fire thrashed and raced along the countryside, igniting everything in its wake, killing everything in its terrible path. People try to outrun it, but it is no use; the magical fire gains speed and incinerates all. It is the most abhorrent night in Arkanyan history, and those who try to outlast the hellfire from the Jigocrugya as long as they can all thought the same thing: It was Rex Separtino who let this enemy, nay, invited this enemy into his doorstep; every claim he made that he was in love was nothing but the result of her spells on him to replace his sense of duty and wisdom with lust and love for the evilest witch who ever lived. Sporadic flares of red, magical cries for support as a last-ditch effort shoot up into the sky as more of the Knights Praer are soundly being overwhelmed.

Massacara is dead. Unlike other stories the children of Arkanya are told about the demise of witches where their death results in the immediate undoing of any and all their spells, no such actions took place when Massacara died. Indeed, it is thanks to her death that Kalypto consumes enough magical blood to cast the Jigocrugya in the first place. Everything she did is to have her steal power so that by the time Kalypto is to eat her, she will have made an impact on his powers and been worth the consumption. Massacara is evil because she has a heart and wants all others to feel and know her pain, as that is the only truth she knows to be unyielding and unwavering—that life is painful. Kalypto, on the other hand, is evil because he willingly, out of hatred and rage, chooses to obliterate any sense of his humanity. He truly is a monster in the fullest sense of the word. It is only that he once used to be human that he can still talk. Otherwise, he will be a mindless, conscious, undead being.

Kalypto slithers through the air, wearing his smoky form in the color of white tonight to mock the merits of goodness, making fun of truth and virtue and beauty. The red fire reflects on him even from the thousands of miles away it is from him, and the smallest tinge of a grin appears there on his horned and malicious face. There is nothing that Kalypto cares for or about anymore. The only thing on his mind is destroying as many lives as he possibly can. The more the better. Not only will he be feasting later on the entire population's happiness, but he will also take such relaxing pride in the fact that his one true purpose has been fulfilled at last. You see, as Kalypto gazes upon his greatest work, slowly experiencing hearing damage from the deafening screams of the death of Arkanya, he believes it is beautiful and good. It is good that so many people now see what he knows— that anything good doesn't last, that anything good can bring more pain than any curse, and most profoundly, that all happiness "is a damned illusion which must be extinguished," as he yells to himself.

Far off in the northeast, Mage Yidnar runs as fast and as hard as he possibly can, but eventually he has to use more magic as the Jigocrugya begins searing and roasting his feet. He uses magic to conjure enough arms to hold the three children, and he uses even more magic to fly rather than run toward the Tree of Fayte. Together the oldest and noblest of wizards in all Arkanya soar through the air like a brilliant orange meteor or shooting star.

"You will not be lost forever, my people. You are all loved, and the dark will end! You must have hope!" Yidnar lets down a rain of his magic, which helps calm the only people left—those who live in the Palacorn of Earth. He lands on his feet using the staff for balance, and the children now look to be between seven and ten years of age. Their development rate is incredible and peculiar but not important at the time. Yidnar levitates himself to survey the progress of the Jigocrugya and sees that not only is the hellfire dangerously close but that they are not alone, and that Earth is the last remaining untouched lands. To his left is the revolting army of the Yamirzen skeletons—eyes of spiders, arms of swords, teeth of roaches, and worms as tongues—a true horrific and blasphemous mockery of Adonai's creations. They make hellishly unidentifiable noises rather than speaking and swarm toward the children. To his right, the Jigocrugya forms like a great trio of snakes and darts toward the children. Dantiel Brea, with his ruby eyes, attempts to use his magic to put an end to this torment, but his and his brother's magic is nullified now. The residual power being this close to the Jigocrugya is too great to overpower by such newborn wizards.

Yidnar uses magic of great power in two different spells at the same time. With his very eyes, he casts the strongest protection spell he can muster—an impenetrable shield around the children—and he then also casts, bursting through the ground of Earth, enormous rocks to form a wall preventing the horrendous army and fires from coming in. He holds onto this magic as hard as he can, but he knows he won't be able to maintain it forever; the army goes on as far as he can see, and the fire reaches the opposite side of the island nation to the shoreline. He is outnumbered, outmagicked, and he cries, slowly realizing this will be his last stand most likely. As he begins to sweat, the army has begun overpowering the barricade, and large chunks will rumble and crumble off, destroying the wall chunk by massive chunk. Yidnar's heart glows orange as he says to himself, "I don't care what they do to me, just please, Adonai, help me protect the children. Without them we are truly lost." Yidnar's tears swell and roll down his cheek, catching the hellfire's light below and acting like glitter as he weeps, trying to protect the only family he has left. The disgusting, revolting, stinking demonic skeleton army laughs and laughs at his acceptance, they assume, of defeat. The fires swarm and roar to the rock wall as well, attempting to melt down the obstruction. Some of the skeletons have climbed upon each other, attempting to scale the wall and throw each other to the other side, and Yidnar, with yet a third spell, shoots fireballs at each fool who tries this. He is panting and exhausted but can't, for every fiber of his being, let anything happen to the children. They are the only family he has.

He swallows his fear and lands on the highest peak of his wall and charges his staff with all of his own magic. Every drop of his enchanted blood goes into the staff (not to be confused with his statute blood, which is the source of life). The staff hums with the overpowering effects, and Yidnar faces his creysons one last time.

"My boys, heed what your mother said to you tonight. Be kind, have strength, and always have love in your heart. I am going to give my life to ensure you three are okay. When I cast my spell, you must hold onto one another as tightly as you can and do not let go until it ends. Please don't forget who you are or what your destiny is, and remember you had a wonderful huge warm family who died for their love for you." The children cry as there is nothing they can do to help, and they watch the sad but awesome sight of Yidnar sacrificing himself for their safety.

Yidnar whispers something in the ancient tongue of Arkanya using the staff Fayte has granted him, and suddenly the ground shakes violently like a great rumbling quake, tearing apart the dirt floor, sending everyone off their feet; buildings collapse, and some of the skeletons fall off the edge to the oceans below as the section of Arkanya called Earth tears and rips itself away from the rest of Arkanya and levitates, rising high above the country toward the clouds until it is out of sight. Yidnar sends his magic from the staff to the floating island in the clouds so that it will maintain itself without his help. He hears the soft voices of his creysons in his head say together, "Thank you, creyfather. We love you, and we will never forget you." He can't tell if he is hoping they said this or if they somehow are telepathic and told him themselves. Either way, he weeps a single tear of love. As he opens his eyes again, the skeletons have surrounded him, and the fire has reached his vicinity. Suddenly, it dawns on Yidnar that the terrible army is not conjured from nothing; they are what the magical reversal of the Jigocrugya has turned people into. *What a terrible curse*, he thinks. He has no magical abilities, and so he uses his staff as an enormous club, spinning around and knocking skulls clean off the vile army. He fights valiantly. They have severed one of his hands off, and he continues fighting for his country, for his wife, and for his creysons. Miraculously, Yidnar's brace fires up a red flare with orange embers into the sky higher and brighter than any of the other flares from his guild. Only one Knight Praer is left to answer the call. Yidnar's life is fading, and his magic is completely gone. His magical glow has disappeared, and all he has is dying hope that someone will help him. He takes more stab wounds entirely through his body from the Skrall Army, and he screams with the pain, unable to defend himself with his consciousness slipping. He collapses to the grounds and is sweating profusely, so close to the purple fires to end all goodness.

Finally, shouting and grunting as he fires four to five arrows at once, killing as many of the despicable Skrall as he can, Zer Raphael rushes to Yidnar's aid. He stumbles with the Arkanya quake as the ground moves like stormy seas, and the Palacorn of Earth rips and tears itself with Yidnar's magic from the rest of the world and floats ever higher.

"Yidnar, stay with me!" he shouts, wanting his friend to live.

"It's too late. Remember your oath. Use the Heatherlyn flower, find the heroes, stop the demons, get out of here. Adonai bless you and our, home." Yidnar has lost so much blood he is pale as a ghost and strains hard to look up at Earth floating away from this fiery hell on Arkanya. "I love you, my creysons." Yidnar weeps and sighs his last breath. The staff from the Tree of Fayte dims to normal dead wood and breaks itself in two. Zer Raphael cries, mourning the loss of his friend and holds him tight. He has his next orders, and he has the enchanted flower still, but he needs a minute. He has lost his wife, his children, and his friend. He stands up, pulls his hood over his face, and whispers into his hands, cupping the magical Heatherlyn flower and, in a flash of blue-and-purple magic, vanishes out of thin air.

*****

Meanwhile, Broque and Bonmal are arguing in the dungeons as they are assigned to guard the potion of Nauz. As a reminder, the potion of Nauz is the potion whose appearance no one knows, for if anyone is unlucky enough to be sentenced to its fate, it boils and disintegrates and permanently removes the magika blood cell from the person who drinks from it. This is only the punishment of a wizard or witch who breaks any of the three laws of magic and is found guilty.

"What in the blazes is going on up there, Bonmal?" asks Broque as they march past each other, patrolling the vault entrance as instructed.

"I don't know, but it can't be good. Chunks of ash and smoldering dirt and grass keep falling down. It must be a forest fire," replies Bonmal.

"Shouldn't we take a look then? What if someone is in danger and needs our help?" replies Broque, growing frustrated as he thinks that Bonmal will reject this cry for action.

"That was not our order! Why do you always have to do something against our orders? All you're going to do is get us in trouble, and I have a wife I need to provide for," Bonmal exclaims. He has had enough.

"Fine! Stay down here and keep marching, like a machine! I am going to take a peek to see what the hell is happening up there!" As soon as Broque props open the trapdoor, he wishes he hasn't. The sight, the smell, and the pain of breathing the "air" is unthinkable. There are no sounds at all. There is no fire, no battle, no nothing, just green hazy air thick with poison, black tar dripping spikes sticks in the ground like murderous spears instead of trees, thousands upon thousands of heart-wrenching corpses burned and charred to a crisp in their final moments, protecting their wives, their husbands, brothers, pets, their loved ones. Everyone and everything have died Broque can see. The ground is black as night and peppered with ash of burning flesh falling from the air. He chokes and coughs on the toxicity that has become Arkanya and closes the trapdoor.

"What the hell was that? What happened?" asks Bonmal, now more concerned with what just moments ago enraged him.

"I don't know, but everything is dead—the grass, the trees, the people. Nothing is left alive. I have to go check on my wife! I have to know if she's okay!"

"*No*! No, you can't go up there, Broque. I won't let you! We've been friends for decades. You can't go up there. Ask yourself something! Arkanya had magic in its soil. How and who brought about this much death? My guess is that whoever did this is still out there!"

"Smart, for once," growls a low tone, raspy, despicable voice.

"Who's there?" they both ask the now pitch-black tunnels. The firelit torches on the walls have burned out suddenly, filling the room with a smell of sulfur and killing their only source of light. Bonmal shivers and freezes in his place as black ice covers his body from his heel to the top of his head, same with Broque. They cannot speak, move, or do anything but feel the imprisoning cold ice that has replaced their skin and is slowly, very slowly, killing them.

"Who am I? Why, my delicious little soldiers, I am the victor of Arkanya, and you will never see the light of day again. You will never again know the warmth of a woman's touch, the smell of a home-cooked meal, nor the feeling you love when you are walking along the beach. No, dear boy. *I will instead feast on your happiness and show you how hollow and deceitful joy is!*" Kalypto laughs maniacally, and his booming evil voice shatters the tunnels as he digs his enormous, cursed claws deep into their hearts, grabs their souls by the scruff, and chomps down like he is eating a chewy steak. The two soldiers scream in fear as they are alive while being feasted upon. First, though, they weep and weep, for the happiness they have felt till this moment is personified by Kalypto's magic and then devoured in whole. Kalypto doesn't have eyes, but if he does, they will have rolled to the back of his head with the rush of power each of their happy souls gives him. The sad thing is they never see him coming, are powerless to stop him, and he can only devour one soul at a time. Kalypto slithers through the air and, as the inhuman specter that he is with blood dripping from his razor-sharp claws, floats through the vault and steals the potion of Nauz.

*****

83

Meanwhile, Yidnar is making good progress, smacking off the skeletons' demonic heads like he is playing serious baseball. He uses his blessed sight one last time, though, and tries to verify that the children are okay. He is bludgeoned on his shoulders, but he keeps his sight. They bash his kneecaps, and he yells with pain, but he keeps his sight. He finally, through his excruciating pain, can see them, and they are safe and holding each other tightly and sailing through the clouds farther and farther away.

His last words are "I will always love you, Liefadra, Ayton, Trang, Baelac, Coragio, and Puretia." As Yidnar is beat and attacked and battered, he has tears of joy, and love, and a final smile. For no one but he can see. The ghosts of everyone he loves are with him, holding his hand as his precious life slips away until he finally cannot take more and passes away. He looks up from the ground, now a ghost himself, and takes his wife's hand, walking once again with his dear friends up to the heavens with the love of his life.

The skeletons at this time have broken his staff in two, are laughing like a pack of feral hyenas, and Yidnar's sight vanishes. The jackal moon turns as blue as the deep ocean, and the stars weep, mourning the loss of such a valiant hero, the wizard who lost everything but continued to fight to protect his family. There is no one left but Kalypto, who is atop the tallest tower in the Palace of the Falls, overlooking the great expansive country now covered completely in fire. He smiles and says aloud, "I am the one true victor of Arkanya. This is for you, Mother." As he rejoices over his achievement in the extermination of an entire population, the fire quickly goes out as fast as it has incinerated the nation.

# 15

## Kalypto's Arkanya

Debris of burned vegetation, people, and materials rain slowly like a demented weather storm brought by a reaper. The air sizzles like meat searing over a firepit, the ground is black with Massacara's tar from her bombs, and the rivers glow eerily green with their lust for death and toxicity. As Kalypto floats through the land, he isn't happy or pleased; he is stoic and fierce. He believes his spell simply reveals what is true versus turning everything on its head and then killing it.

He grows more and more violent as he sees the few things struggling with all their might to stay alive—a small family of birds huddling together, gasping and choking for air through the thick tar, feathers seared and their nest sinking. Kalypto looks down and smiles, laughing as he walks away, not ending their torment but rather snapping his fingers conjuring a pedestal to rise out of the water composed of skeletal arms with hands together forming a bowl, trapping the birds to forever struggle and be close to death but never die. As he floats throughout the air over flowers that haven't been seared, they wither away to shattering ice as he passes. Then stopping him in his tracks, he sees people—families and individuals dismembered, some missing organs or limbs or layers of skin from the flash fire. They have no energy or ability to scream, so it is quiet, but the choirs of pain on their faces are deafening. The passion in their dying hearts crawl as close together as they can so they won't die alone, the sorrow some of the individuals have until the families who don't even know them in life huddled together; the state of affairs is bleak, burned, and abysmal, and it fills Kalypto with pride. The air is quiet but not still. Seeing so much as one person alive, though, is enough to make him want to cast Jigocrugya again.

Kalypto slithers along, smelling the air and grinning. It is like the smell you get when a candle has just been extinguished, only the entire world is ablaze, not a small votive. One by one small group-ings of survivors are discovered by Kalypto, and he doesn't summon a huge army to kill them, nor does he use magic to eat them like Massacara. Instead, he converses with each and every single surviving Arkanyan. He doesn't use magic to pause time either. He doesn't care how long it took; he gives everyone his complete, undivided atten-tion as he drives them all to suicide.

In Kalypto's skull, he is innocent. All he is saying are facts; it's not his fault that people choose dramatic responses. Can you be cer-tain though that his very words are not hexes? That his gaze is not a trance? There are fewer and fewer who can.

Kalypto kneels, meeting the foolish survivors of the Glorious Fire (as he will forever refer to this day) at their level and speaks but three sentences to each of them, one by one.

"What is your happiest memory?" Kalypto asks a survivor. They cannot speak, as their mouths have been broken, but Kalypto has no patience for disobedience and simply gazes at the poor person. They suddenly have the ability to speak but immediately let out a scream so terrible he cannot maintain, and it fades to a cry. Whatever the poor soul is remembering, likely his wife or family, are dead. The sorrow of missing the source of his happiness is more painful than both of his missing legs and his burned flesh. He looks up at Kalypto, tears stinging as they mix with blood on his face.

"Please, have mercy, just kill me," begs the suffering survivor. Kalypto completely ignores his pleas.

"What was the unhappiest time of your life? Oh, so sad, my child. Too many to choose from?" With the end of his second sen-tence, Kalypto looms in close to the poor man, face-to-face on the ground. This whole time, Kalypto has taken the form of this man's best friend, until now. Kalypto morphs with swirls of his deceptive smoke-like self and transforms into a copy of what the friend looks like now, completely destroyed by the disasters and terror of the Jigocrugya. The poor man weeps and weeps until he has no tears left and is just screaming to himself.

"Please, sir, please kill me. I don't want this," the man begs again. Kalypto stays in the form of his dead best friend and grabs the suffering man by his neck and forces him to look at the destroyed and dead world. He screams as his body can't take the pressure of using muscles that no longer exist, bones that have been broken or sprained, and flesh that is gone.

"You did this. You brought this with your lies of hope and your deception of joy. Your whole life is a lie, which makes your soul meaningless." Kalypto kicks over a dagger from a nearby dead soldier.

The poor man will have wept more if he can but sees the glint of the blade and lunges it far into his chest, ending his life and misery. Kalypto laughs a hellish chuckle as he floats away, the fire behind his skull glowing red and billowing out of his eye sockets. Every chuckle is a deep, raspy grumbly, belly laugh that shakes the ground and chills the air. He reaches the shores of what once was Earth and stops. He uses as much magic as he can and tries to decloak any spells on this area. He never remembers such an expansive ocean breaching the border of his country before. He swiftly flies from side to side using magic to discern what the hell happened. His vision, though, enhances by powerful, dark magic, grew fuzzy, and he feels pain as he struggles to see. Suddenly, he sees in his enchanted, cursed vision. He can just make out what look like two glowing orange wooden rods.

# 16

## Aftermath and the Stranger

The good people of the Earth Palacorn are all but befuddled. They have just experienced the most violent of magic ever in the history of their world. But as much as their hearts desire reunion with their families, so too do they seek answers to their burning questions. Buildings have collapsed, homes are destroyed, but there is not one death, thanks to Yidnar's magical specificity. This is to say that when he used the Staff of Fayte to sever the Palacorn from the rest of the world, he also at the same time cast a protection charm on each of the citizens so they won't be killed in the actions.

It is a hot, blaringly sunny day as the surviving corner of their land are hiding above the clouds and closer to the sun than normal. The crowds begin to get louder and louder as tension and confusion grow more and more. No one has any answers to anything, for nothing makes any sense. There is too much pain and not enough light. And most troublingly, the people *do* remember the details of the late Yidnar uncovering the most fate-filled prophecy, including his belief in three mysterious brothers who are the only chance anyone has for survival in Arkanya.

The people of Earth begin panicking into a frenzy, a circus of one-track-minded mammals clamoring for answering, cleaving onto old hopes, and refusing to listen to any answers they don't want to hear. Most of them are badly injured, in shock, or have lost so much blood they can scarcely stand. The section of the land held up entirely by a dead man's spell is an enormous chunk the size of most average-sized countries, and this is just a sliver of Arkanya.

"What has happened to us?"

"How do we get back? *Can* we get back?"

"What happened to Arkanya? What happened to our Palacorn?"

"Are we being attacked? What if whoever it is comes for us?"

"Where are the supposed heroes? If anything, I'd say the whole thing was a ruse to have us blind! Have us all distracted looking round for heroes when our doors are open to attack!" The people of the Earth Palacorn are enraged, confused, hurting, sad, and excited. The rush of energy they feel is in direct response to being the only living things left of Arkanya, or so they think.

*Where are the heroes, indeed?* the three brothers think. Can the prophecy actually be true? Are they really destined for such greatness? *Not likely*, they all think. They want it to be true because otherwise the death of their family will have all been for nothing. The only hero they know is Yidnar, and he has sacrificed himself for their safety. He suffered a horrible death but did not mind, as he truly believed with all his being that they are the true heroes the Propheta Fior speaks of. Baelac and Ayton are concerned. If they are the heroes, surely, they have much to answer to "why didn't you stop all this," "how come you let this happen," and the like. And likewise, were they not the heroes, then their creyfather, Yidnar, and their parents all died for nothing.

"No. They didn't. We may not know who we are, but everyone who loved us died for us to ensure we had a chance. We can't let them die in vain," Dantiel says. Yes, the three brothers can talk, walk, think, remember, and do an abundance of things not normal newborn babies can. *Babies* is a very loosely used term here as the children look visually to be twelve years of age, no less. The mob-like crowds grow more anxious and more raucous as time goes on due to their desperation for immediate answers to their questions and for some kind of absolution they fear they are unable to get.

The three brothers huddle together and feel fear; the crowds are blaming *them* for all that has transpired.

"It's your fault they're dead. Aren't you supposed to have magic? Where were those fancy spells to save us all then?

"Yeah! You just sat around and let the world burn! How do we know they aren't the true villains? Get them!" The crowds of raging and fearful Arkanyans race toward the three brothers who immediately begin running for their lives.

"What the heck is wrong with these people? We are actually babies. How could we have cast this spell to bring the end of the world?" asks Ayton.

"It's not the end of the world, not even the end of only our world. Look around you, Ayton. We are still here, they are still here, and the wretch who started this and murdered our family is also still here. What does that tell you?" replies Baelac. He has much wisdom for just being a day old.

"This is true, but it doesn't explain how and why we're able to walk, talk, run, and other things. We are only a day old! My point is we need answers every bit as much as they do. Let's try to reason with them!" Dantiel says.

"He's right we can't run forever. That' not going to help anything. Come on, let's stop here and turn around. We have to face the music."

The brothers wait until it is almost too late as they near the edge of the world. The mob catches up with the three brothers but are confused as to why they stopped running.

"What are you doing? Why have you stopped?" one citizen asks. In the background, silently, a hooded and cloaked person slowly creeps in the shadows, keeping watch, out of sight and out of reach.

"We can't run, and we don't want to. We want the same thing as all of you. Our family was murdered right in front of us, by the same witch that murdered the High Archon. I am telling you, we are not the villains here. We have only been here for a day and are orphans. Our creyfather kept you, all of us, alive because he believed in us. He believed in this," Ayton stands on a platform for his moment and holds out the Propheta For, which promptly illuminates via magical projection the full prophecy as transcribed and decoded by the late Yidnar. Flashes of colored light speak in the ancient, now unused, tongue of Arkanya and show images of all that have transpired: the murder of the High Archon, Rex Separtino, on the Balcony of Defeat at the Palace of the Falls, the genocide at the Rexa's coronation, the betrayal of the Lord of Malice, and finally, the Jigocrugya. At its conclusion, the Propheta Fior has fulfilled its full purpose and dims to appear as a perfectly spherical marble.

"If you don't believe us, look over the edge, but be careful," states Baelac. The people of Arkanya lean over and saw the charred remains far below of their home world. Some scream as they imagine the torment and terror their loved ones must have experienced leading up to this. Many others gasp and fall completely silent.

"You will listen to what we have to say, everyone!" shouts Baelac, addressing the remaining population. Ayton looks saddened by the true horrors of what their home has endured in just several hours.

"This is not an ordinary charm or spell that was cast. The Jigocrugya is unknown to us, yes, but what we do know are the facts. It burned every tree, person, and animal in its path. But that's not all. It also spawned a terrible army of misshapen skeletons and insect hybrids that slaughtered everything else. There is no one left. We are all there is. But we must have courage! The prophecy, which was true about the fires and therefore must be true of the salvation, foretold of three heroes, brothers born in the month of Idamay. I don't know if it means me and my brothers. In some ways, I don't want it to be because this quest to save Arkanya is going to be confusing, terrifying, and dangerous, and some of us may not survive, but it matters not. Whether it means specifically us or not, we will fight. We will protect and defend you, and we will get our home back!" Baelac exclaims to cheers and approval by the Arkanyan folk. Widowed mothers grow worried, and everyone feels something they have not felt since months ago—hope for a brighter future. Now they have a chance. But is it legitimate?

"That's an awfully great speech, but how can you deliver on your promise? It only took one of whoever it was that ruined our homes. To me that means whoever it was has much power. How can you hope to defeat them?" a citizen asks. The hooded and cloaked person approaches the front of the line.

"We have magic, and we will learn as much as we can to hone our skills and become powerful warriors. We cannot do this alone. We need help," Ayton explains as his eyes glow bright blue as he steps into the light beside his brothers.

"How can you be so sure it is you? What if the true prophesied heroes were killed overnight like everyone else?" asks the citizen. The hooded and cloaked figure looks around searching for someone or something.

"Because look at us. We were born yesterday," Dantiel says. Some laugh at this, as it does sound funny but obviously is also true.

The hooded figure, lurking in the back of the crowds, swiftly alters his attention to the brothers upon hearing Dantiel speak of his age. He knows of only one group of people this will be true for, and his hope grows.

"We cannot guarantee that we are right. All we have is what we know right now, and everything points to the same thing. I'll be honest, I am not so sure it's us either, but I can't risk that if it is us, we just sit down idly by while the specter is still out there. We have to try. But like my brother said, we can't do it alone. We are unskilled in, well, everything, and we need help."

The hooded figure approaches the three brothers, sliding off his hood and untying his cloak, revealing a beautiful emerald-green tunic, high-top brown leather boots, and a strong bow and quiver filled with feathered arrows on his back. The mysterious man has jet-black hair down to his back and a small strand of braids on his left side. His skin is lightly scarred from battles fought before, but his sword arm is strong and his shoulders confident. Around his neck is a totem of the creator, clearly a man of faith. On his right arm, he wears a large copper and marble bracer.

"Look into this flower and tell us all what you see." The mysterious man shows his back to the crowds only. The three brothers do not know or trust this man and are alarmed at how close he has gotten to each of them.

"Who are you?" Ayton asks.

"Answer my question first, and then I'll answer yours. Disarm your magic. I mean no harm. Your father was very close to me. You all have my loyalty. It's an honor to meet you three."

The three brothers realize the flower in the man's hand is but a Heatherlyn rose from the meadows of the same name in the northeast. These are the enchanted flowers that show a glimpse of either your past or your future. The man is brilliant for prompting the brothers to look into it, for it will indeed not only answer the questions of whether these three brothers re the prophesied heroes but also assure the people of Arkanya. The crowds smile, loving the sight of such beautiful, magnificent parts of their home before the Jigocrugya. The flower glows and stretches its blue and violet petals like a child waking up in the morning, stretching their arms. As the brothers stand and slowly, apprehensively, walk toward the strange man, they look at each other, nodding it is okay to do this, agreeing this man startles them but they have no choice, and they are there for each other if something goes wrong. One by one, the brothers gaze into the flower, and the Heatherlyn flower glows blindingly bright blue and pink, growing in size and floating before them. They wince as they hear cries of the people of Arkanya dying by sword or by fire, families ripped apart, their souls being stolen, and innocents being mutilated.

When they gaze into it, the crowds weep and cry as the fires of the Jigocrugya with occasional identifiable faces are killed. Then, magical and brave images of Yidnar's final moments—sacrificing himself for the safety of the children as he uses every bit of love and strength, he has to endure the torture from the Skrall Army encircling him. Then, they see the one thing they think they'll never again: scenes of the death of their parents by Massacara's deception and darkness. Their mother's last words urging them to "have strength, be kind, and always love" echoes in their heads. Finally, the Tree of Fayte appears with the rivers of the Lake Souviens glowing at its base. The tree speaks: "Behold, for these are the brothers I have foretold. They must accept their destiny as pieces on the board have already begun moving in this game of chess. There can be but one winner. Beware! The Lord of Malice has captured and hijacked the very nature of Arkanya, including it in his reversal spell of Jigocrugya. All that was good, beautiful, and helpful now has become deadly, ugly, and foul. Be strong! Remember who you truly are! For once you return to Arkanya, everything will want you to fall. Worry you not, 'tis but evil shall rot." And with that, the three brothers faint and black out on the stone floor of a ruined temple.

# 17

## The Mundane vs. the Extraordinary

The three brothers are not harmed, but they have just been shown the previous day's events, and the idea that they are the three prophesied heroes are once again instilled within them. They stress about the challenges they'll likely face, assuming that the enemy who brought their world to its knees in just a few hours will want to make that look like child's play compared to what he must intend for them, and they fainted. So too do they think of the profound duty they may very well be sworn to follow in the coming time. For a one-day-old, this is highly overwhelming. Nothing makes a lick of sense. Why are they aging and developing so fast, will it stop, or do they not have enough time to figure things out? If it is true these three brothers are heroes, then why? Why will one random villain seek the destruction of their parents so fervently? The brothers know nothing except that they don't have any options and finally have someone trying to help them. The stranger, on the other hand, has a clear agenda, one he frequently checks to ensure he is still on track. What that agenda entails though only he knows. As he approaches the blacked-out brothers, the crowd steps backward to give him more room.

Some of the people approach the stranger and say, "If you hurt them, we will truly be lost forever in this netherworld above the clouds. Be truthful or leave us." It is not a threat but fact and a request for a guarantee that the only rumored possible help will be protected. The stranger lowers his brow and nods in confirmation.

The stranger equipped with the bow and the Heatherlyn rose brings the three brothers to his wooden cottage deep in the only remaining forest, affectionately named the Penultimate Forest, as many dwellers of this floating Palacorn still hold onto the hope that one day someone can save Arkanya.

For weeks, the stranger cares for the young lads, nursing their wounds, teaching them history, math, and other important subjects. The three brothers have yet to be mentally stimulated in such depth so the fact you can see the gears turning in their heads is every bit as much astounding as it is a sign of relief that the stranger's teachings are working.

Every day that the stranger with a copper-and-marble bracer teaches them new skills is another day one or all of the three orphan brothers ask angrily who the man is and why it is so important to him that he help them. Every day too is another day their answers are brushed aside with an ominous comment, "Your answers will come when I know you to be ready. Not before and after it's too late. Come! We have much yet to learn," the stranger will reply. The skills they learn varied immensely from cooking and fishing and forest survival without magic, to hunting and craftsmanship for making a shelter out of mud leaves and bamboo, to combating with their bare hands and feet, to learning how to manipulate magic with their eyes closed to sense without even looking where a threat lies.

"This is foolish! How am I supposed to see what I can't?" asks Ayton and Dantiel. Baelac watches from the side as he practices with a bow he has just carved, conjuring in a mist of green-and-gold light a full quiver of feathered arrows.

"A true hero of Arkanya does not need to see! Have you not heard of Arkane Tauriel? He was so attuned with the innate magic of the world he could cast spells without moving a muscle. He never once flinched, and you can bet he was terribly afraid! Come on now, son, the fate of your home depends on this!" Ayton and Dantiel are sweating, the use of so much of their magic now also exhausting them physically. Panting, stinking, and salty, the sweaty brothers try harder and harder to accomplish what they think is impossible.

"Stop, stop, stop!" cries out the stranger, wiping sweat from his own brow. Is he too using magic, or is he sweaty from the hot summer day? "This is wrong. Magic is not an intellectual equation to untangle like a maddening riddle. Think of who you love, think of why you are doing this, and more importantly, who you are doing this for. Focus on that, and I guarantee there's untold miracles you can perform. Now try to strike me. Don't worry, I can block. Now, attack me!" The stranger runs back to his training position in the field, and the people of Arkanya line the perimeter, watching the moment unfold as if they are at a sporting event. What they witness is far greater.

The stranger attempts one more time to strike Dantiel with Ayton blindfolded and hands bound. Immediately, Ayton's back illuminates blindingly bright blue, and he floats high above the ground and conjures from his heart an impenetrable shield protecting his equally blinded brother. The crowds gasp, and the stranger cheers, claps, and encourages the audience to follow suit. The event is far from over though. The stranger now uses this as an opportunity to attack the non-included Baelac who is still focusing on honing his bow and arrow skills. With just a few inches to spare from piercing the brother's neck with an axe, Dantiel and Ayton together form a glowing blue-and-red-winged serpent as large as the ancient oaks long gone. Dantiel's back now also look like a great red sun shining through his clothes and floating above the ground with his blindfolded brother.

The crowds cheer and gasp in a great emotional and spiritual pendulum swing of awesome feelings. The stranger weep with joy, as he knows more than anyone else in the sliver of the rest of the world, that he is indeed in the presence of the victors of Arkanya.

The brothers float gently down back to Earth and open their eyes, taking each other's blindfolds off. They see their backs shining immensely and take their robes and shirts off, exposing to the amazement of all, something incredible. Baelac's mouth drops, and he joins his brothers. As soon as he approaches them, his eyes and back follow suit, glowing bright green. He too disrobes his tunic, and as each of them holds each other's hands, gargantuan, ethereal shining wings the color of their magic spring magnificently out from their shoulder blades on their backs and extend for twenty feet in both directions from their sides.

The stranger approaches the heroes and is so impacted by this astonishing moment he weeps with joy that the prophecy is true.

"Behold, my friends, I am Zer Raphael. I am the last surviving member of the Knights Praer, a guild your creyfather formed for the insurance of your safekeeping and the resurrection of our home and the preservation of its future. Sworn like a guardian angel to protect and defend you. Yidnar was right. It is you!" The brothers weep as well. Finally, there is something they cannot deny that not only unites them but also gives them confidence there is indeed a fighting chance to save their home world and avenge the fallen population. They hug each other, looking up into the sky, thanking Adonai for this chance to take real action to save their home.

# 18

## The End of the Heatherlyn Rose

After a time, the hoopla and ballyhoo have died down, and the Arkanyans return to their daily task of building shelters, caring for the sick and wounded from the Separation, and tending to their own families as well. The three brothers are feeling a kaleidoscope of emotions. They are elated with an enhanced sense of self-worth from the magical achievements they just achieved, but they also feel terror and stress now, realizing that the Propheta Fior is likely a true and real philosophy, meaning the fate of the world and everyone in it rests on their shoulders alone. They also feel a sense of confusion. Yes, they may understand that it is real, but why? Why them three in particular and not anyone else in the world? And what is the significance of Zer Raphael? The stranger who has been caring for and tending to the three brothers Ayton, Baelac, and Dantiel has *finally* revealed his true identity as Zer Raphael, Knight Praer from Mage Yidnar's guild.

"The answer to that question can only be answered by the one true Cry, Adonai" replies Raphael. "Pray on it, and he shall answer you in his own way. Fret not on things you cannot change, my friend, for life is full of woes and challenges, so there's no sense in worrying about what cannot be undone. Instead, use that energy for something productive and that can help yourself and others. It is not unnatural that you might feel undeserving, or that you might be questioning why you and your brothers among all the rest, but that is not for us to decide. Pretend, for instance, that you got your answer.

What would that change? Assuming it wasn't another crazy ideal that disturbs you such as this, what would you do? Anything different? It matters not the why. It matters the how and when. The people of this world have only one hope—that the rumors of a prophecy being the only source of a voice speaking hope for the end of darkness is true. No, we cannot raise the dead, nor can we go back in time to undo what has been done. Which leaves only one option. You must at some point return to Arkanya, face the villain, and defeat him. It is the only way this can work," explains Zer Raphael. But is it truly a guarantee that with the death of the strongest wielder of Yamirzen magic, it will be enough to end his spells? With only a few months of teaching, even Ayton, Baelac, and Dantiel do not believe that.

"How are we supposed to do that?" asks Ayton.

"That's up to you. No one has ever even tried before, and the thing about the Lord of Malice, the Prince of Evil, is that he isn't human. His magic is unpredictable like his very nature, and he has no conscience, no morals, and no heart."

"No heart? How is he alive?" asks Baelac.

"He isn't," replies Raphael. Baelac and Dantiel exchange skeptical glances and laugh.

"Did I make a joke? You of all people should understand this. He destroyed the world and is responsible for the death of your family. Have a little decency and respect before ridiculing your own history, imbeciles." Raphael is greatly aggravated and walks away, not wanting to further become angry for their jokes over the death of his friends and their own family. The brothers simply do not understand, nor do they believe that such a beast exists and are convinced another explanation has to be the answer. Surely, they will not be asked to kill someone. And how do you kill something that isn't human? Baelac and Dantiel know something terrible has happened; they are not fools, but they are at the same time not of the belief or understanding that the culprit is some sort of ghost monster that wiped away a world in the blink of an eye. Everything about the monster seems made-up to Baelac and Dantiel. From his visual description to his abilities, none of it is believable. He can understand if Baelac and Dantiel are in denial of this truth, as it is so horrible they won't want to believe, but this is different. To be so convinced as to not acknowledge the full scope of the dire situation they are in is negligence at best, blind and grossly ill-prepared at worst.

"Well, you know what, I hope you wake up soon because at some point, you're going back down there, and if you're not ready, he's not just going to kill you. Actually, technically he hasn't killed anyone. What he does is far worse," replies Raphael, who has stood from his seat and is gazing toward the edge of the world. He is annoyed that something so obvious to him is not believed.

Ayton hears the conversation but chooses instead to simply pay attention from a distance and is climbing a nearby tree.

"What could be worse than death?" asks Dantiel.

"I know you're still very young in reality, so please close your eyes and imagine something for me. You're alone, isolated from everyone you know who makes you feel wanted and makes you feel safe. You are approached by someone, whose mere presence makes you incapable of controlling your motion, yet you can feel everything. Imagine an invisible layer of ice covering or perhaps replacing your very skin. You're in pain just by existing, and then he kneels down to you, a juicy, dripping skull floating in a spectral mist of stinging haze, and he speaks to you. With one sentence he reminds you of some of your greatest memories. After the second, you feel like all of that was fake, hollow, and false, and at the end of the third…" Zer Raphael turns away, not wanting to even think about it but turns again to face them as this is legitimate and necessary for Baelac and Dantiel to fully understand the level of threat and level of what's at stake as well as the risk involved. "At the end of the third, you do yourself in." He can tell they don't understand what this means. "It means you kill yourself. That's why I said he technically doesn't kill anyone, but you must not brush this aside. This is only as of yet half over! Pay attention! Your father and mother endured ten times worse than that! Listen to me!" Baelac and Dantiel are joined now by Ayton as well. They sit down together and listen to the only person whom they can trust, the only person who knows the full scope, having fought the monster before, or at least fought his army. Ayton hugs his brothers for comfort. The reality of this tale for him is frightening.

"Your parents faced what not even most of Arkanya had to—his special ability." Raphael closes his eyes and weeps, being reminded of the grotesque sights of this on the battlefield only a month ago. "So I told you before he only speaks thrice to you, and typically the victim attacks themselves fatally. Sometimes, though, when a person or victim is strong enough, happy and faithful enough, they can resist the magicked urge to strike themselves. It is only in that moment that the Lord of Malice can, with either of his six-fingered claws, dig into your very soul and tear it almost completely away from your body, pluck out the part of your soul that stores happiness, memories, and love and consumes it as if it were a steak dinner. Do you hear me? He eats part of your soul! Your parents, bless them, were so strong not only did they resist striking themselves, but they fought Massacara as she tried to eat their souls. Ultimately, he was too much, and they could not overcome, but you need to know that is the monster running free in your home, that is the monster who brutally destroyed your family, and that is the monster who rules over Arkanya now. Take some time to process this, but when you're ready, take this and watch it together as brothers. It may answer your questions, but trust me, if you're a good person, you'll have more, and then I want you to come find me." Zer Raphael walks away back to his hut and leaves the three brothers huddled together, processing what they are just told. Magically appearing in a swirl of gold glitter, a single large glowing lilac and magenta Heatherlyn flower appears in Baelac's hands. This is the same flower that introduced the brothers to Zer Raphael, and it has but three petals left; it has one more thing to show and tell them before the end.

# 19

## The Return

Brothers Baelac, Ayton, and Dantiel huddle together to determine the best course of action and to determine what the Heatherlyn rose has just reminded them of. The moment they pluck the final petal from the bud of the rose, it flashes brightly and shows each of them a glimpse of their birth followed by the deaths of their parents from the deceit of Massacara. It shows how and when their parents are visited by god Adonai himself who established the validity of the Propheta Fior and blesses them with a gift to have every birthday moving forward be a day the monsters have no power at all. The rose also shows when their parents ask Yidnar to be their guardian and creyfather. It goes forward to also show the sacrifice and death of Mage Yidnar, how he risked it all to ensure the safety of the future of Arkanya and to ensure the protection of his creychildren.

The brothers are quiet and solemn, wanting privacy within which to reflect upon the duty that lies before each of them, along with the choice that duty presents itself to them as.

"Do we drop everything and risk it all ourselves, fulfilling what we've been told time and time again is our prophesied destiny to save the world? And how in the hell do we save the world? Logistically, what does that even mean? Infrastructure? The people of Arkanya are dead; apart from the survivors on Earth, none had survived the Jigocrugya, or whatever it's called, and no amount of magic can bring them back. It's just not in the cards. So what does it mean to save the world? Kill the monster that caused all of this?" Ayton has a million big questions as he tries wrapping his mind around all of this. Baelac is silent, thinking about everything.

"Oh yeah, sure, a bunch of two-day-olds go up against, 'the strongest wielder of dark magic the world has ever seen.' What could possibly happen there? Do you hear yourself? So what! We can fly without an object or make shiny stuff appear out of nowhere, but what use is any of that against a monster like him? It's useless. There's nothing we can do. We're just kids. I mean heck, we're infants, newborns!" Dantiel rebutts. He isn't wrong but not entirely correct either. The weight of it all is beginning to crack the glass-like fragile support of their limited understanding of the situation they are in.

Suddenly, Baelac stands up. "Not another word. Do you hear me?" He picks up the petal again from the large and now dimming Heatherlyn rose, which continues to show the scene of their family's death as if on repeat. "This is the answer to everything. *Yes*, it is true there's a magical beast thing down there in our home, which is the absolute, strongest sorcerer ever in existence. Oh, you don't believe me. Peek over the edge and tell me if you see any life! Any at all, and I'll shut up. None, eh? Okay! *So* we established that as the fact that it is. What's next? Oh, right. Why us, right? Adonai himself chose us! Why? Because our parents loved each other more than anyone else in the world! They loved us so much that before we were born, they asked, of all people, Mage Yidnar to be our creyfather to protect us and our future. Did you think it was just because they were best friends? No, it was because Yidnar understood how to decode prophecies, and he knew that one right there was going to come true. If *everyone* believes and knows it to be true, how can we do ourselves, our home, our own parents such a betrayal of not following through with it? Do you want their death to be in vain? Because inaction, to do nothing, is to slap our family in the face. To do nothing is to say it's okay that our home is destroyed and that almost an entire population is gone. It is up to us, and it is going to be scary and tough, but there's a reason why Adonai chose us. I don't know what that is yet, but that's what we have each other for! To protect defend and support each other. No matter the threat, no matter the cost, no matter the situation. Are we good? Everything make sense?" Baelac has spent ample time reflecting and thinking to have processed everything he just explained to his brothers. In order to come to that state, however, it means he had to find the right headspace and clear his mind of all doubts, suspicions, and feelings, to listen to the facts. Whenever something stressful comes up, it is often most advisable to pay closer attention the facts however few they may be. Facts cannot lie, nor can they be bribed or stolen. Facts can be like stepping-stones across a lake of confusion to the shores of confidence. He tries to explain this to his bothers as well, and Dantiel again points out their youth as an excuse to not follow, to which the boys laugh, and Baelac says, "Age is but a number. We're living proof, you two and me!" They nod and walk in stride with one another, off to Zer Raphael's hut to tell him they believe, to tell him they are ready to return to Arkanya.

They trudge through the overgrown, untamed Shimmering Forest along the trail Raphael has shown the boys once during their magical combative training.

"Guys, just to be safe, we should arm ourselves. You never know who may be watching," says Ayton. The veins in his hands glow blue as he charges his palms with a spell to bring frostbite to any opponent. Baelac's eyes glow green to allow him to see farther and farther to alert ahead of time, and Dantiel's feet glow bright red as he conjures miniature meteors in his fists, ready to explode upon impact with an opponent. The brothers are armed, strong, faithful, and ready. But what is to come they can never be prepared for.

It appears they have been walking for hours though only one has passed, and Dantiel believes they are lost. He refuses to bring this up though so as not to raise tensions in an already tense situation.

"Perhaps we need directions," says Ayton. Dantiel sighs.

"No, we are following the path Raphael showed us just weeks ago. Come on, it ain't much further."

"Or we are missing a turn and traveling in circles," Dantiel finally states. Baelac sighs and then his hand glows green. He kneels and places his hand on the grass. Not only is his magic recharging, but he also chooses to manipulate magic in such a way that their previous footsteps illuminated bright green to show them the way.

"How do you know those footsteps are from the day we walked to Raphael's?" asks Ayton.

"Good call! Dantiel, give me your hand," asks Baelac. Dantiel kneels beside him, and he channels his magic to use the stars as a chronometer to dictate and shuffle through the footsteps and now only illuminate those which lead to Raphael's hut from that last day they made that trek. Ayton snaps his fingers at a shrub nearby and transforms it into a freshwater spring. They all take a drink in the summer heat and thank him. Ayton dips his hand in the water and recharges his own magic like what his brother did on the grass.

"There, now we have a path!" states Baelac, and they continue walking. Suddenly, there is a branch that snaps loudly in the distance. Baelac immediately snaps to look in each direction, searching for the source.

"Well done, kids," a voice hiss.

It is one of the few members of the late Skrall Army, Kalypto's final remaining disgusting soldiers that has scurried over the border to Earth and been swept up during the Separation. Malnourished and with their thirst for blood unquenched, they are desperate like feral wild animals, foaming at the mouth at a new opportunity. The brothers have no idea what in the world this creature is, but one can rather easily discern where its loyalties lie.

It lies in the grass and coughs and wheezes, begging for aid.

"What do we do? Obviously, this thing isn't on our side," Dantiel says.

"And what led you to that conclusion? Its appearance? Come on," replies Baelac.

"No, Baelac, he's right. Look at him. He has marking all over his skin. Are those runes? You're not even natural. You were made by someone. Who are you and where did you come from?" Ayton asks, arming his palms, which billows snow and drips frost, with his eyes' glow intensifying.

No answer from the creature apart from a sickening worm-filled grin and bubbly, gross laughter.

"I know who you are, Ayton Brea!" hisses the creature. The brothers can now tell it is armless.

"How do you know my name? Speak! Unless you'd like to be ice for the rest of your life, unable to die and unable to live frozen between worlds!" Ayton threatens. The gross creature coughs up roaches and worms. He is already dying but hates the idea of not being able to.

"All right!" he coughs more. "All right! I'll tell you. I am number 7,325. There were eleven million before me who stormed your world. We were created with a sole purpose—to destroy everything. But there was one among the rest, a lion among sheep. He carried a large wooden staff and clubbed me and used great, strange orange magic to defeat me and several others. But my friends surrounded him, and we won! That's who I am, *I killed Yidnar!*" hisses the vicious creature. The brothers are temporarily stunned by this revelation. One part mortified, one part astounded by such a small world, and one part furious.

"Oh, you should have been there to see it! Ha!" He laughs and coughs up his version of blood. "He wept and wept thinking he wasn't saving you three. Well, either that or the fact we'd already chopped his leg off!" He laughs again with his gross, gurgling voice. "But don't worry, we killed him fast after that. Who knew, Ayton, who knew that one person could endure so much torture and blood loss? But he did. By Kalypto, he did" Almost instinctively, Ayton and Baelac cast their first combative spell. Ayton encases the vile creature in ice, and Baelac conjures a tree to grow from out of the demon's chest. The magical ice keeps the creature alive, and the tree prevents the thing from doing anything but, well, being a tree. The trunk of the tree bears the creature's dying face, and birds immediately claim this as their home. Ayton blasts the tree with a blizzard and creates a new kind of tree, a snowy willow. The tree is white as snow and will never grow.

"So he's the one," says Dantiel. "He's the one who killed Yidnar, our creyfather. Why did you make him into a tree? He deserves no remembrance!" he cries.

"We did not make him into a makeshift tombstone. We turned something horrendous into something beautiful. I just want to make sure we don't end up like the very thing we hunt." Ayton answers.

"Oh, did you rip its soul out and eat it? Did you attempt to murder its babies? How about light its entire planet on fire? Did you do that? I'm pretty sure you're not even close to the kind of demon that piece of crap is!" Dantiel is angry and hurt.

"Dantiel, calm down, brother. It's going to be okay," Ayton says.

"No, it's not! Our whole family is dead, and you just framed the murderer!" Dantiel is beside himself.

"I promise you, we will show the monster no mercy, but that creature, that thing, does not deserve to take part in that action. What we did was suspend it from any afterlife to forever be an inanimate object. And trust me, that is not merciful. Just try to relax and not focus on wanting to kill so much. This isn't about revenge. It's bigger than that. It's bigger than all of us. And we have to stay in the light if we are to extinguish the dark." Dantiel wipes his tears and nods in agreement. Baelac raises his eyebrows, impressed that Ayton isn't wanting revenge.

A few more hours walking, and the three brothers finally arrive at the hut belonging to Zer Raphael. Through the trees and over an old wooden bridge that traverses a fish-filled stream, the cottage has a round stone roof with a short, stumpy chimney billowing thick smoke out of it like an old politician smoking a pipe. River rocks and beautiful oakwood cover the walls and foundation of the cottage, and the floors are hardwood as well. Plenty of windows with flowing curtains and light illuminate the beautiful yet simple home, and there are glowing crystals in the ceiling for additional light.

There is something delicious-smelling cooking over the fire in the kitchen, and there in the living room stands Zer Raphael, tapping his fingers, waiting all this time for the three brothers to finally arrive. He is tapping his fingers on a pile of large stone boxes, each one a different kind of marble. One is midnight blue in hue, another forest or emerald green, and finally the third has a pink-reddish tone to it.

"It's about time you showed up. Apologies, my conjuration gave you trouble, but I have something for you three." That is it! Raphael conjured an illusion of a dying Skrall Army member. Ayton and

Baelac laugh vigorously, noting in their heads how Dantiel reacted to the encounter.

"Ha, very funny," Dantiel sighs and chuckles as well though.

"Take the box that speaks to you and meet me in the study. We eat after your final training." Zer Raphael turns on his heel, carrying his own black-and-white box clearly made of marble and walks down the wooden hall toward the study. The three brothers study the box and try carrying it like Raphael so easily, but it immediately crashes to the floor with its deadweight. Confused and annoyed, they have to figure out how to carry it without carrying it.

# 20

## The Challenge of the Box

The brothers each tries to simply use magic to levitate the box, but to no avail. They try helping each other lift with brute strength, also to no avail. The struggle becomes confusing and rather annoying to figure out, and suddenly it dawns on Dantiel.

"Wait, guys, hold on here. What do you notice about these boxes?" he asks.

"Besides their weight?" asks Baelac, sweating.

"Yes, besides their weight. Look at 'em! They're blue, green, and red"

"Okay," says Ayton.

"It's a puzzle. They're color coded to our magic! Remember what Raphael said. All magic has color, sound, light, and temperature. We need to use the magic unique to each of us in order to move them," theorizes Dantiel.

"That's actually a strong point. It is likely not a coincidence that these are color coded for us. Let's try it," Baelac says.

Ayton stands up and stands back, charging his right hand to throw a blast of water at the box, and not only did the box glow, but it also immediately floats and hovers gently above his right hand.

"Whoa!" they all yell. "Don't drop the spell. You'll lose a toe!" Dantiel exclaims. One by one they each charges a hand for magic and carries the boxes without touching them. Well, all except for Baelac who comedically chooses to enchant his head to carry his box there rather than above his hand. They march down the hall and meet up with Raphael who is waiting for them in a large, empty, windowless room.

"Finally. You boys are taking your time for everything, aren't you? Okay, now that you solved that riddle, open them." Raphael sits down and, in seconds, conjures an armchair before he hits the floor, and in a blink, the black-and-white box pops open with a loud bang and a silvery cloud of glitter. Once the dust settles, a rare form of armored robes wait for him. "Oh, and you lot will likely have to fight your boxes in order to open them. Just a word of advice, give each other some space." Raphael conjures a cup of some clearly delicious beverage while he waits for them to begin let alone complete their next puzzles and tasks.

"What does he mean fight the box? Who would ever fight with a box? That's the most ridiculous," Dantiel murmurs under his breath, and as soon as he charges his other hand with magic and gestures with his glowing hands to open the box, something happens. Dantiel, in a thick, red fog, disappears!

"Hey! Where'd he go?" Ayton and Baelac run toward Raphael, but he points at the box.

"Each of those boxes provides a unique challenge only each of you can solve. No two challenges are alike, and you can't help each other. They are incredible blacksmiths once you complete but trust me when I say the reward is hard-earned. Have no fear. Your brother will come out victorious as will each of you. Now go meet your challenges head on! Face your fears! Defeat the trial! I'll be here when you finish. And then we can eat dinner. Good luck!"

Ayton charges his whole body, opens the box, and an enormous wave engulfs him and brings him inside the box.

Baelac charges his arms and legs, and a large tree forms, scoops him up, and brings him inside his box too.

The three boys are each faced with a unique challenge only they can match just as Zer Raphael says. But what he hasn't told them is how long it will take to succeed. For days, Ayton struggles to constantly cast a water-breathing spell while also fighting a half octopus guarding a castle. The giant squid sprayed ink and roars, calling for additional aquatic foes Ayton must defeat. Or so he thinks. On he fights the monster of the deep, and the squid has not only caused damage to Ayton but also to nearby reefs, which are densely populated with innocent undersea life. Ayton charges both of his hands with magic and decides a new tactic. He wants to disarm the opponent's desire to fight, not kill him. The beast resists such attempts, but eventually, Ayton's spells to change his target lands straight at the octopus's head. Suddenly, the giant, tentacular fish bows its head and sinks to the ocean bottom dead. The task is not over, however. Ayton uses magic to restore the reef to its former glory, and the fishes return to their homes. Suddenly, there is a blue, loud bang and flash; and still soaking wet and covered in seaweed, Ayton is sent back to the real world and waits for his brothers.

Baelac is pulled to a haunted forest he must cleanse of darkness from. Evil ghouls and dark ghosts wisp throughout the trees, spreading fear and stunting the growth of wildlife and vegetation. If left unchecked, the entire lands will die and burn. It is up to him to protect different forms of life other than his own, and so Baelac wanders throughout the forests. Each tree begins to enclose their branches, attempting to entrap him, snakes appear where sticks once lay; and shrubs shake off their leaves, revealing rabid wolves. Life is ill and needs purifying light. Some wolves snips at his legs and draws blood and Baelac's returning strikes land fatal blows. Baelac at once snaps his fingers in both of his hands and begins pollination season of all the vegetation, plants, and trees. Though Baelac is allergic to such pollen, the act allows the plant life to rehabilitate themselves and revert back, with the help of his natural magic, to their original, pure state. The new season blows away any magic that is not his own. As time passes, the animals stop in their tracks from chasing him to eat him or worse. The wolves are tamed and form a pack and go off to go find shelter from the storm, the vultures above stick to their squadron of three and fly away, and the trees cease trying to trap or harm Baelac, and some thank him for his aid. Grass grows where once there is only mud, and the lands turn into a beautiful forest full of life. The tree hand that brought him here also sends him back, and Baelac conquers his box.

Dantiel is faced with a peculiar challenge. He sees an alternative version of himself, except one who is depressed and hates himself. On the skit goes, and eventually Dantiel sees his doppelganger approached by none other than Kalypto, no not the real one, the visage of him produced by the box. Dantiel can't make out any dialogue, but at the end, he remembers what Raphael said about Kalypto's special strength: inciting self-afflictions. So Dantiel uses both of his hands and conjures a beautiful, starry night sky filled with everything he loves: meteor showers, shooting stars, and the borealis lights. The doppelganger of Dantiel weeps and weeps, and just as he is about to do himself in with magic, he looks up to wipe away his tears. The real Dantiel uses magic to actually write with stars, "do not yearn for the stars, you are one," telling himself to love himself rather than hate. The doppelganger stands up mightily and conjures an enchanted sword made from the ice of a meteor and cuts clean off Kalypto's smug head. Dantiel conquers his box and is sent back to the real world. All of them have passed out upon reentry to the real world. As time has passed so much, they have begun to age while in the box world, but upon coming back, returned to their real state, Ayton vomits Baelac passes out, and Dantiel sleeps for almost a day. It is a taxing challenge that takes time and more constant expulsion of magic than any of them has been asked to use before.

"Well done! Well done, each of you. You see, I told you. Many people in Arkanya have magic, but only you three have your branded tricks and skill sets. Now approach your box and say, 'Ra zul.' Okay, say it with the pause," instructs Raphael, who snaps his fingers, drying off Ayton. As each of the boys says the magic words, their boxes shake and explode in a bright blue, green, and red cloud. Once the smoke clears, armor perfectly matching their dimensions lays on the floor:

Ayton has a metal breastplate attached to woven silver-and-sapphire threaded cloak embroidered with gold leaf and beaded with larimar stones. Larimar stones are native of Earth Palacorn and are a beautiful light blue color, so colored by their natural creation underwater.

Baelac's box explodes in a lime-green mist and once that clears, he has a mint-green and mahogany-brown tunic with chain mail. The tunic is predominantly brown, woven with silver thread and dipped in the rich reddish-brown color, embroidered with bright and bold minty green patterns native to Arkanya and beaded with diamonds.

Dantiel's box explodes in a pile of sparkling red sand. Once it blows away, there on the floor for him is a suit of red metal armor, red in two shades—dark red nearing black with red tints and bright red like fire. All of their armor is due to how they fought and how they behaved during their respective challenges. They all don their magical armor and join Raphael at the front of the room.

"My goodness, I think we earned the hell out of that, don't you?" asks Dantiel.

"I mean, I feel like that whole thing took both four years and an hour at the same time, so yes! But it was very disorienting. I learned a lot though. I learned that it's important to kill for self-defense, of course, but there are so many other factors to consider like collateral damage, any innocent people nearby, etc. Very helpful," Ayton agrees.

"I'm thankful we have Raphael. That was very kind of him to grant us the opportunity to be challenged by these boxes, not just for the reward which is going to be greatly helpful but for another challenging and difficult experience using magic and working on problems if we are separated. I think that's really important for us just in case." He looks at his brothers and has a small smile on his face, one of care but also of concern. If they return to Arkanya and are separated, there needs to be some assurance that they'll be okay on their own, for the first time, in a world with everything trying to kill them, and they're only a few months old.

"Have you all noticed something else? We haven't been growing at an alarming rate anymore. When the world ended—" Dantiel is interrupted.

"It didn't end. It's still down there. It's just reversed. Everything beautiful and helpful about it is now hideous and deadly. Important difference," Ayton corrects.

"You are correct. Any ideas as to why?" asks Zer Raphael.

"Well, I would imagine it's because the Propheta Fior is correct, that we are the prophesied heroes and that it is up to us to bring the light back to Arkanya. We have decided we believe it to be true and that we not only should but also want to do our best to undo the Jigocrugya. I don't know what dangers may lie ahead, but if there's anything I've learned these past few months, it's that no matter what happens, we're never truly alone. The people we love who are no longer here with us are not gone. They have simply moved on to a better, simpler world, away from all these tribulations and wars. But we also always have each other. We are brothers. Nothing can ever stop that, and that is what connects us. In a way, Raphael, we are connected to you too. You are the closest thing we have to family besides each other now. You kept us alive, you helped us believe and understand, and you protected us, gave us food and shelter, and above all, knowledge. For that, we are eternally grateful. We wouldn't be alive without you. You have been our guardian, our chef, our teacher, mentor, parent, nurse, everything. Thank you." The other two brothers join Ayton at the end for thanking Zer Raphael and agree that they too are ready to return to Arkanya.

"You know, that really means the world to me. I believe so much that it is true. The things I have seen and experienced all tell me that. I was the first person whom Yidnar knighted in his guild for the sole purpose of doing what you've just said I've done. I cannot follow you back, but I will always be with you. Should you succeed, you'll see me again. I promise you that. Now come here." They all hug, and Ayton is emotional. This is indeed the only family-like person they have left, and there is no telling what will happen once they get back to Arkanya. They hug for a moment, each one wanting to begin an eternal pause, to just enjoy this moment instead of getting ready for the next, but that is not the way of the world. For, in all of our lives, while it is important and paramount to live in the now; to appreciate the calms before the next storm, it is equally important to not quell responsibilities, and the three brothers have the greatest responsibility of all.

With that, Raphael is first to break the hug and bids them all to follow him to the familiar edge of the world.

"You're kidding, right?" asks Dantiel.

"The only way down is to jump," instructs Raphael, albeit very nonchalantly. The three brothers exclaim loudly as they are miles and miles above Arkanya, ten miles to be precise.

"Now I've given you your enchanted armor. It will allow you to fall from any height without taking damage, but you must use your magic to control your fall. Use it to slow your momentum and come to a rest as easily as you lay in bed when you reach the bottom. Repeat that after me now!" The brothers repeat and are terrified. "Take these crystals. They'll automatically slow your momentum if you panic and don't do it yourself. Stuff them in your pocket so they don't fall out."

"This is crazy. Are you serious?" asks Dantiel.

"We already know your magic is unpredictable in this world," Ayton adds.

"This is also our only option! There are no flying spells. We don't have time to teach you how to use a broom, and there are no portals now until light is restored in the land. This is the only way. Now, once you're down there, trust nothing. Trust no one. Have confidence that the only things alive, should anything be alive down there, are in fact trying to kill you. The plants, the air, the water—everything will be targeting you. So you have to be aware, you have to be quick, and you have to be smart. Never take off your armor for a moment. It is essentially magic on autopilot designed to adapt to any environment to the best of its ability. Trust only each other. You have one mission: defeat Kalypto. Once you do that, Arkanya's magic will be restored, and I can join you. If you land in different places and you get separated, your first mission is to save and rejoin with the missing brother. *Never leave another behind. Got that? Never.* Once you find the missing brother, keep trying to defeat the Lord of Malice. Stay alive. Trust no one and nothing, stick together, and defeat Kalypto." Raphael cries with worry. These children, though they looked like twenty-year-olds, are only six months old in reality.

"Are you ready to go back to Arkanya?" he asks as they swallow their growing fear.

"Yes," they all say in unison. Just then, up in the sky way above the clouds, the sun shines brightly and warmly just for a second and then goes behind the clouds again.

"One more time, never leave one behind. Keep trying to defeat the Lord of Malice. Stay alive. Trust no one and nothing, stick together, and defeat Kalypto." They nod and stand at the very edge of Earth fifty-five thousand feet above Arkanya. "Jump." And all three jump.

# 21

## Fear, Rage, and Dust

The three brothers take quite literally the largest leap of faith they ever have. Beginning their descent from Earth is a modest fifty thousand feet high in the sky. For reference, there are no birds that fly this high, no mountains in Arkanya this high, and no forms of life as the air is too thin, and there is not enough heat. Journeying back to their home world after just six months of Kalypto's unchallenged reign of terror over Arkanya, the brothers are petrified with fear. They are completely free-falling from higher than anything in the world. Down below, the closer they grow, more and more things ever so slowly come into focus in their vision: The lands are black as tar; trees are like splintered toothpicks, half broken and leafless; the rivers are a lime green likely with poison; and there are no beasts or animals of any kind, at least not from seeing forty-nine thousand feet in the air. The brothers link arms to attempt to guarantee that they'll not be separated, but even that is no great insurance policy. Magic is as dark as it can get in the land they are approaching. Who knows how the only sources of light magic will react to such venomous, vile hexes?

For as much as Kalypto wants to obtain what he finally has, one can scarcely see why. After all, he is the only High Archon to rule without any subjects, without any cabinet members, and with no one around but his millions of members from the Skrall Army. Oh, and of course, Massacara's rotting corpse.

Down the brothers fall, now approaching roughly forty-five thousand feet. The air is still cold, and though the air temperature begins to rise slowly, none can tell from the generous upward breeze they feel with their fall. The brothers are all so worried about the other. Their faces are hard to see with their eyes watering as the wind blows everything up. With their free hand they have to cover their nose and mouth to make inhaling effective, and there is nothing connecting them to anything, no rope, no hooks or cables, just them and air. That is it. The fear of the unknown in each of them shall they be on the ground at this time will have been enough to stop them in their tracks. Dark magic is painful, horrendous, and has no restraints. Indeed, it is why the three laws of magic exist and, some suggest, also why the enchanted Lake Souviens exists—to banish any wielders of it. Still, the brothers have nothing to do but wait to see what will come next. Luckily, they have a fail-safe in the form of the fall-stopping crystals that Zer Raphael has gifted them before they jumped. Even with that though, what if he isn't to be trusted? Surely, he won't have pushed them off a cliff being in cahoots with the greatest villain of all time. Why will he have trained them with his skills and knowledge of magic?

Down further still, they plunge at an incredibly fast and increasing velocity fall. This is one of the most intimidating experiences of their lives. To realize that every second they quickly approach not only possible painful death, but even if they survive, they'll be placed in the single most dangerous area where its very nature is magical and catered to trying to kill them—the air they breathe, the animals they may see, the flowers that bloom, the water that flows in the rivers, everything trying to kill them or stop them or both. It is scary and completely unavoidable. They, by virtue of still free-falling, can do nothing at all to stop this. Suddenly, an unpleasant experience become exponentially grimmer.

"Where's Ayton?" yells Dantiel. All this time, they have been linking arms to prevent this, and yet it somehow still happened.

"What do you mean? Oh my gosh, he's gone! Dantiel! Do not let go of my arm!" In a horrifying explosion of blood-red flames, Dantiel also vanishes from thin air, leaving only Baelac behind, who is furious. *How could I have let them slip away,* he thinks. He needs to get down on the ground. Enough with this infernal falling where he has no control of anything. *Wait,* he thinks, *I have the power to control nature. Let me try the nature of my fall combined with the crystal to essentially appear safely at the ground level.* So he takes the crystal, smashes it in half against his armor, and drinks the dust from each half. Gambling he can create his own magic, he uses the crystal dust to cast the spell, and then, in a green flash of flames, he too disappears.

There is a series of three incredulously loud booms, each one a few seconds after the previous, and each one emanating from different sections of the land. The booms kill the silence as abruptly and fervently as the fires have extinguished life from this ashen wasteland. The booms create magical shock waves, sending visible waves of some force, blowing and knocking away anything within a five-mile radius of each collision's impact with the ground. The ground rests for a brief moment after the third shock wave, and then there is a great rumbling and quaking deep within.

Far south, deep in the shrieking mountains, there lies a foreboding fortress. Each black marble turret is as pointy as a witch's hat and as shiny as her daggers. It copies the silhouette of the surrounding mountains, making it damn near impossible to locate until you accidently happen upon the front gate. Statues of winged beasts belch flaming oil perpetually and spills directly into the nearby branch of the former Eirini River. This is Kalypto's fort, and deep within the castle walls, he sits on his throne, which he stole from the Palace of the Falls. There he sits and grimaces, reveling in his unstoppable power, his intelligence, and his ultimate victory. The walls and ceiling of the palace are covered in not any ordinary mirrors. Each mirror covering the walls is once a citizen of Arkanya. Kalypto takes pleasure admiring his success and achievements but enjoys snacking on the trapped souls of the reflective, innocent lives each mirror contains. Over the months, the mirror people rust with tears as their family and friends are destroyed one panel a day, every day. Kalypto will approach one of the mirrors and admires himself for the better part of a day and then tires of it and digs his enormous razor-sharp claws deep into the center of the mirror, which ripples like a pond when a pebble drops in it. Out he'll rip away the soul, filling his home with his favorite sounds—screams of terror and the sobbing of those left to witness. He smiles widely as he feasts on the shiny, cloudy, mass of the soul he tears out. One evening, as he sits upon his throne and ponders how his wretched father can never dream of accomplishing all he has, the floor of his palace erupts in a series of deep, rolling rumbles shaking the castle thrice. He explodes the mirror in his hands, melting it into liquid silver and staining his massive shiny clawlike blood. He arises from his rusting throne and illuminates the fire within his skull as dark red as blood.

"What in the blazes was *that*? No matter, it won't last long." He grins as he ruins the stone halls as he exits the palace. His hands wrestle with each other, eager to destroy and hopefully eat the soul of whatever caused the rumbles and disturbances. The Lord of Malice is seething with rage. How dare someone or something have the audacity to disturb his victorious, delicious slaughter. Kalypto begins hunting for the source of such callous annoyance. He holds out his claws ahead of his billowing, foggy self and uses his dark Yamirzen magic to scan for any sources of magic. The fire burning inside his skull roars and rages loudly, glowing behind all the cracks in his bones and rushing out of his eye sockets and open mouth through his many fangs. On he scans with his magic until he finds something. To his shock, horror, and volcanic rage, he detects another source of magic. One he cannot, for some reason, translate as easily as all others, one he feels only when he finds Yidnar's broken staff.

Meanwhile, the three brothers' worst nightmare has just been realized. Each one lands safely, sure. But that's where the good news ends. They are beyond disoriented, eyes watering still from the fall, hearing muffled from the suddenly changing air pressure, and Dantiel finds himself growing angrier and angrier. He has fallen in what is once the Heatherlyn meadows. The former charming and beautiful roses, which gleam in sunset ambers with their blue and purple petals and grant the people of Arkanya glimpses either into the future or the past, are now black flowers shaped like tined, razor-toothed jaws, like a Venus flytrap but with actual teeth. They belch a pestilence of thick, foggy green haze, which causes Dantiel to cough and to hallucinate false memories in his mind. False, perverted memories of his brothers beating him up drawing blood and slapping his face, false perverted memories of Zer Raphael strangling him in the night as he tries to sleep, and memories of Yidnar attempting to kill him as a baby. He can't any longer tell if they are real or not, but everything around him chants, "Kill them! Kill them!" while laughing periodically. Dantiel screams alone in this haze of deception; the flowers all around him grow taller than trees, and some others remain small in height to tie and twist around his hands and feet, trapping him and forcing him under their maleficent influence. Dantiel cries with the emotional pain as the flowers actually get up to his face and laugh at him, mocking his agony and jesting with his torture like a pack of hyenas. The haze is beginning to increase in intensity, and Dantiel's eyes bleed, being polluted by such black magic. The flowers have released him, but now the haze has convinced him that staying is better than being with such vile "family." He can barely remember Raphael's parting words, "Trust nothing, leave none behind." He can hear it echo as if it is a sole person shouting in a crowded sports game. He tries to get up but when he looks down, he sees that he is aging, faster even than when he was born. He moans with the settling arthritis and shrieks with the whiting of his hair and hunching of his back. He groans as he tries to traverse the cursed meadow, but even trying to crawl is excruciating. He pushes through the pain though his mind keeps telling him to stop. He starts succumbing to the magical influence and wonders if everyone he loves *has* tried to kill him in the past and that he shall have instead killed them. Further, the Yamirzen magic coaxes him into believing that everything he needs is in this one meadow, bidding him to never leave. The skull-shaped flowers rage on, enticing him to move faster and faster, hurting himself more with every crawl and step. They drive him mad with their strong convictions of contradictory messages. His skin is covered in liver spots, his hair and teeth begin falling out, and alas, he can move no more and collapses to the ground. The vile flowers laugh in their hideous, high-pitched shriek of a laugh and surround him. Dantiel lies motionless and exhausted. He can barely remember why he originally wants to move and feels he has more reason to hate than to love his brothers and is content to stay.

Suddenly, in the distance, a figure through the thick, green haze can be discerned in the distance approaching him.

*****

Baelac lands a second after Dantiel, and his first priority is to reunite with his family. There is no telling what horrors the three of them may have to face and no guarantee they can handle whatever come their way. Baelac immediately charges his entire body with his natural magic, illuminating himself green. Needing to somehow track his brothers, he remembers how he and his brothers found the hut belonging to Raphael. He kneels on the gross dirt and mud placing his palm deep within. Something in the ground blasts him back with a magical red explosion of repulsion. It seems the very nature of the new Arkanya does not agree with light magic. Baelac is left to hunt for his family the old-fashioned way. He turns on his heel and gazes into the distance in all directions with his enhanced vision but sees no signs of his family. He starts to panic but tries encouraging himself. *Just pick a direction. Keep it moving*, he thinks. Surely there'll be signs or clues of them at some point, but if he stays put, he'll definitely die. He starts walking and then jogging to the northeast from his initial landing spot far in the southwest. He hears another pair of footsteps approaching him from behind, stopping him in his tracks. He breathes heavier, as he does not see anyone else around him. The footsteps press onward, and now he can make out footprints in the mud, chasing him down. He swallows and continues, hoping his stress is making him see things. Whoever or whatever it is chasing him now starts running after him. Baelac refuses to look behind him and runs as hard as he can away from whatever is chasing him. Harder and harder he runs like a gazelle, his stride growing to help him gain distance from the mysterious, invisible opponent. It manages to chase him into the former forest deep in the southwest, very near and within eyesight of the new shores, where once Earth laid peacefully. He looks up and wishes Raphael is with him to help.

He wipes the sweat off his brow and realizes he doesn't hear the second pair of footsteps anymore. Hoping he is finally alone, he catches his breath, leaning against a tree. Or at least what he, in his fearful and tired state, thought is a tree. That the tree is really a giant beast is as much a mind trick as the ghostly running footsteps haunting Baelac. The beast opens his eyes and extends his wings, showing the grotesque hybrid; he is part vulture and part lion. The great wretched beast flies in the air and begins chasing Baelac. Baelac fires bolts of poison from his bow with magic rather than arrows, and he strikes the great, winged creature, crashing him down to the dead ground. He creeps ever so carefully over to inspect the thing, and just as he believes the deed is done, he sighs with relief and wants to continue searching for his brothers. He cannot tell, but the dead trees in the ruined forest around him are indeed not dead at all and spring their roots out from the muddy dirt and trip him. By the time Baelac rolls over to get up, the winged lion has approached him again and gives him the hardest clawed punch of his life. There are three blood streaks deep into his face as Baelac, still pinned to the ground by his foot under the writhing tree roots, remembers his training with the box. He firmly grabs a root with a free but sore hand, and while he knows he can't stop the Jigocrugya's effects, he wonders if he can temporarily pause them. He injects his magic into the tree belonging to the root he grabs, and again the tree refuses his magic and throws him into the air. *At least I wasn't pinned anymore*, he thinks. The beast is well beyond his abilities for now, though, so he runs out of the woods to the north. He is limping and screaming with pain, but also he yells to push through the pain, knowing that stopping equals death. Baelac looks up and, for a brief second, catches a glimpse of the beautiful moon, shining only the smallest three little specks of light amidst her otherwise shadowy dark face. He takes it as a sign that those dots of light resemble the specks of hope he and his brothers represent. He weeps, thinking what they must be going through and is tired of running away from the damned beast! He can't believe it, but ahead of him in the distance far away is the figure of a body collapsed on the ground. Can it be? Is it another trick of the land, or has he found one of his brothers? It is too important to ignore, so he runs harder to investigate. The winged lion is growling and snarling and leaping through the air. It is wounded too but not anywhere near defeated. Alas, Baelac can tell the unmistakable shine of his brother's bright-red suit of armor, that it is indeed Dantiel only he appears to be about eighty years old, handicapped, out of breath, and weak. Baelac theorizes quickly based on his experiences that small geographical sections of this new Arkanya are bubbles or spheres of Yamirzen influence, to mean that this particular zone is one that brings age faster than natural. So Baelac picks him up in his arms and continues running as hard as he can, though now Baelac himself begins to age. He approaches feeling about middle-aged but doesn't let this stop him. Harder he runs, holding his motionless, unconscious brother while he knows the beast is still out there.

"Run!" he hears a voice echo in his mind as he pauses to catch his breath. Can it be Raphael? Or his father? Or maybe he is that tired and weak. Either way, it motivates him to no end, and he runs with the wind. He runs holding his unconscious brother as they both continue to age, almost as if the faster he runs, the faster they age, but Baelac's adrenaline is not to be trifled with. The winged beast lets out a furious growl of rage, having lost his first duel with a meal, and slowly walks toward them. Baelac has exited the dead forest but reaches the edge of a small cliff where again Earth once broke the fall, but now, a hundred feet below this hill lies nothing followed by the ocean. Baelac turns around, and the winged beast has reached him, slowly tiptoeing, sizing up his next meal, licking his chops, but also stomping his paw into the ground, saying "back off, this land is mine, back off." Baelac can tell the beast is mere seconds from charging and decides to play with the half-broken, dead trees. At the very last moment, he splits a fallen tree trunk in half, wedging the beast between the logs and holding him. Baelac, still holding his brother, approaches the great beast and sees the great beast tire of struggling and settles. He speaks to the great, winged lion.

"You will not defeat me! I came here to save this world. Look at this land. It was your home too, and now it's dead! You will cease your foolish attempts to stop me, or I will end you. It's such a pity, really. If you hadn't tried to kill my brother and I, I'd say you're actually in a way, a beautiful, forceful creature. My purpose, however, is too important, and I cannot let you continue to stop me. I will let you free only if you choose to never again harm me or my two brothers. I will kill you now if you lie. You know I can. I clearly have magic. You are a slave to it, aren't you? Tell me what you prefer." Baelac offers the beast release from such an existence or the freedom to carry on shall he change. But can he truly be trusted?

The beast coughs and chokes on blood but replies, "You put up a greater fight than anything I've hunted for months. But I am sworn to kill you. If you have honor, you must destroy me. My kin and myself are only created to end the three babes should they have survived Jigocrugya." The beast has an unusual tone, raspy and deep yet also sort of old English and proper sounding.

"You know of the Jigocrugya?" asks Baelac, mildly confused.

"Do not insult my awareness. I wouldn't be some monstrous, unnatural hybrids were it *not* for the Prince of Evil."

Baelac grows frightened. What else can that person, monster, thing do? He doesn't understand anything except that he is in danger, danger which every moment magnifies.

"Freedom is yours should you wish to change. But if your choice is death to no longer be a slave to someone else's command, I will oblige. No one should ever be a slave to anything," Baelac replies. He is surprised that he is talking to a winged lion who, moments ago, tried to kill him but now understands that the beast has no choice.

"You seem like a nice man, but you're too late. Forget about me. If you truly have come to save this horrid land from the magical prison we're all in, then never stop. Fight until you win, but beware, he knows you're here." The beast begins choking more and coughing up blood.

"Who? Who knows I'm here?" asks Baelac.

"The Lord of Ma…" And with his last breath, the beast has officially completed a change of heart just by speaking with one of the three destined heroes to save the land. Baelac, without even trying, has accomplished what only the folklore speaks about the Drakulogons of old: speak to animals and heal them from curses. The beast lets a single tear drop down his orange-and-bronze fur and passes away.

Baelac bows his head, thankful for his assistance and final warning. Who on Arkanya can he have meant though? Perhaps the second pair of footsteps that began this mess, or something else entirely? Time is quickly running out, Baelac is convinced. The world is enormous, yes, but so too is his desire to find his third brother. They have been out of the cursed meadows long enough that the aging effects have cleared away, and Baelac runs out ahead, growing tired and weary from traversing and trudging across lands that all the while try to kill him. He trips and drops Dantiel a few times, but each time, he picks him up and keeps running. He uses magic again to increase his speed and in the green, hazy distance sees the unmistakable former Lake Souviens. Once proud and beautiful, it is now black like paint and bubbling like lava. He can make out the distant echoing sounds of splashing and thrashing like something struggling in the water. He drops Dantiel beside a tree and casts a force field to protect him at the banks of the lake and is now close enough to see the horrific sight of his second brother, Ayton, fighting without magic, Skrall Army guards drowning him and beating him to a pulp. Baelac rolls up his sleeves and tries to recharge his magic but again is blasted away by red fires from the Yamirzen soil rejecting his light magic.

"Okay, gonna do this the hard way." Baelac dives into the black tar-like lake and is instantly horrified by images of his dead family rotting and decaying, screaming profanities and trying to tear him limb from limb; others try pulling him down. He knows these are all fake though, and just as he starts running low on air, he kicks with all his might knocking clean off the heads of each of the fake, magical corpses of his parents and Yidnar. He swims hard to the surface and gasps loudly as he finally swallows air again. He approaches Ayton who has lost a lot of blood and is now motionless as the Skrall keeps whaling on him blow after blow. Baelac fights valiantly while also trying to float, which is difficult and exhausting. He has spent all day, trying to find and save his brothers, only to find each of them seemingly defeated. The voice of either his father or Yidnar or Raphael has guided him thus far, so he has faith but is low on stamina. He tears off an arm of one of the Skrall and uses it to soundly bash in the heads of the others. He is struck a few times on his back, which makes him swallow whatever this "lake" is made of, but he gets up each time, screaming, trying to muster whatever energy he has left, and defeats the remaining Skrall. He too has lost a substantial amount of blood. He doesn't care so much and is totally oblivious to it, focusing instead on his family and keeping them alive. He is fading in and out of consciousness and has less to no energy left but tries as hard as he possibly can to bring himself back to shore and resuscitate his brothers. With a loud gasp and heavy, fast-paced breathing, Baelac washes up on shore and rolls Ayton inside the force field for protection resting on the banks. Covered in black mud, the tarry substance, and blood, he prays for healing as he uses his magic one last time to extend the force field around himself and sleeps on the banks, totally spent, unable to move, unwilling to try.

# 22

## The New Arkanya Is... Different

Baelac, Dantiel, and Ayton lie on the banks of the boiling, bubbling lake of evil as they attempt to regain their energy from quite a grueling day. But can they or shall they trust the land enough to sleep out in the open? The black ashen and burned scorched lands are interrupted by the brilliant red, green, and blue from each of the brother's magic, like bright stars amidst a night sky. Suddenly, the quiet is called to rise.

In the distance, one can hear a sound reminiscent of the ocean. Baelac groggily wakes up and smiles, thinking it is the lapping of the waves from the lake. When he finally comes to, however, the soil has piled atop itself, forming a pyramid the size of a tree, and with a loud, erupting explosion, mud and clay and rocks are expelled in all directions as the Skrall Army is reformed and begins charging toward the three brothers, according to Baelac's eyes. In a panic, he magically disengages the force field and tries to wake them. He shouts and tugs, smacks their cheeks and shakes their shoulders, but wake they will not. Baelac tries everything he can to wake his brothers, but they cannot overpower the Yamirzen magic's grip on all of them. Remember what the sage has warned: "Trust nothing." Shall you even trust the description of this scene? How can you guarantee the army of the Skrall is storming them again when last we saw they had burned to a crisp as well?

"Wake up, Dantiel! Ayton!" screams Baelac. He grunts with frustration and gives up trying to wake them as the ferocious, feral army approaches him, hissing and growling like hellhounds. He punches the ground with both of his fists, causing a landslide to appear with his magic, and just at the last moment, when the army are to clash swords with him, the brothers wake up and laugh till their bellies are sore.

"What the heck is so funny? Want to give me a hand killing these idiots?" Baelac grumbles as his face is splattered with tar as he kills tens of Skrall.

"Uh, look again, dude," Ayton says.

Baelac is confused. He stops fighting, looks at his brothers, and then turns his glance back at the Skrall, and instead of the disgusting, ferocious mud-dripping skeletons they are, he sees nothing but waist-high burned down trees as far as the eyes can see.

"What in the—" He is intimidated. The lands are playing tricks with him, and now he wonders if he can trust anything. Has he indeed found his brothers, or are they a trick too? After all, they just laugh at his failure.

Baelac grows angry. He conjures magic in both of his hands again, this time forming an ethereal dagger and holds it to Ayton's throat. Ayton chokes and gasps for air.

"What are you doing?" asks Ayton, terrified, panicking, and fearful.

Dantiel is laughing till he falls over.

"Are you truly here, or are you an illusion too? Answer me!" asks Baelac.

"Yes, I'm real. I'm your brother!" Ayton shouts back, coughing. Suddenly, a raspy, deep-toned laugh chuckles, echoing throughout the lands, and a rush of wind soars through the air, blowing their hair and robes.

"We are not alone, brother," Ayton remarks.

"Prove to me you are who you say."

Ayton's eyes glow bright blue and blue translucent wings unfold from his back, levitating him above the ground. "Our mother met our father through their friendship with Yidnar. We were visited by

Zer Raphael, one of Yidnar's knights." Ayton returns to the ground, and Baelac tears up, hugging his brother, sorry he has jeopardized him.

"I just needed to be sure. So much of this world is a lie now," he apologizes.

"You can always be sure of me," reassures Ayton.

Dantiel is taking his armor off.

"What are you doing?" they ask him.

Dantiel turns his head all the way around his spine, which shall have killed him, but it doesn't.

"Clever little rats, tell me, did your parents have the intelligence you applaud yourselves with? How far did that get them?" Dantiel laughs with red and yellow glowing eyes and an echoing laugh.

"Who are you?" asks Ayton. He and Baelac both has armed themselves with magic.

Dantiel cracks open his head and rips apart his body, revealing the shredded soul of the evil Massacara.

"You cannot defeat me! I was sent to hell when I was defeated, but I was too strong to be kept even there! I have been remastered into this form, and I can do so much more than just eat your soul." Massacara's withers and shredded black, red, and pink soul take the form of a silhouette of her former self, a glowing shadow if you will.

"What have you done to our brother? Where is Dantiel?" Ayton runs over to him and cries. This time it is Baelac's turn to laugh hysterically.

"How can you laugh? Your brother is dead!" Ayton shouts.

"Ayton, it's not real. Dantiel is right behind you. Can you not see?" Baelac chuckles.

The cursed, vexing lands of Arkanya plays constant tricks on the brothers meant to either drive them mad or to harm one another. However close they may stray to succumbing, at the last moment, one of the brothers will be aware and helps the others. A vital trio, the three saves each other all day long. Or so it seems. While a week has passed according to the brothers, only an hour it has actually been since they fell off of Earth and returned to Arkanya. The deep, dark spells are thick and powerful and everlasting. As the false vision fades, the real Dantiel is seen crying beside Ayton, horrified that his brothers have tried to kill him, with their false versions of reality spilling into the actual reality. They hug each other, crying from the stress of fighting what turns out to be nothing but black smoke and fog and thinking one of the two of them has been killed.

"How do we trust ourselves? Our eyes? Our ears?" Ayton asks his brothers as they make camp with their own magic instead of natural ingredients.

"We can't. Remember what Zer Raphael told us. Trust no one and trust nothing. We cannot even fully trust ourselves," says Ayton.

"No! The minute we distrust each other is the minute I know we've already lost. We just need a tool to determine where the tricks are and where they aren't." Baelac and his brothers begin thinking of what they can do to achieve this vital task.

"Hey, I got it! We all have magic, right? Raphael taught us many things about how to channel it and use it. One of the things he taught us which stuck with me was that, like magic seeks out like magic. All of us have a similar type of birthright magic—you know, our special talents. What if we use that part of our magic to detect other types of magic like that? We are the only ones here with it, right? Everything else is either undead, dead, or Yamirzen? We can use our magic to detect each other!" Baelac is proud and thankful that his brother came up with a solution so soon. He glances over at Dantiel who is also thankful.

"Ayton, that's genius. We'll do that then," Dantiel says. The three brothers check their belongings and their armor and continue their quest to learn ways to save the world, whatever that means. As they press on past the former Lake Souviens, they approach the meadows where once the Heatherlyn flowers blossoms by the millions. Now black razor-sharp, monsterlike flowers dot the burned lands, with blood-red thorns and bright-orange leaves. The cursed vegetation looks like a crowd of fireballs waiting for a victim to kill. Suddenly, they have three.

As the brothers approach, Ayton, distracted by their dark beauty, sees one in particular that looks like a regular Heatherlyn rose and veers away from his unknowing brothers, lured in by its contrasting beauty. He can hear nothing but his echoing footsteps, see nothing but the one flower getting close, but his brothers race as hard as they can to his aid, but they are too slow in these time-slowing meadows of deception. Ayton has succumbed completely to the curse of the vile flower and finally reaches its roots. He kneels with his eyes as black as night. As soon as he plucks it, his hand turns black and his teeth grow fangs. The flower bids him to keep walking away from the treasonous, "heroic" brothers. Dantiel and Baelac cry and weep as they saw the horrific sight of Ayton tumbling off the mountainside.

# 23

## Run

The brothers yell as their firstborn falls over the cliffside, down almost as far as the Palace of the Falls is high. A fall like that will kill anything. They cry as they can't see from this high up any impact below but feel they know he is gone. All they can do is watch in slow motion their brother tranced by the cursed flowers and fall to his death.

"What the hell do we do now? Why bother doing anything? The prophecy was plural. It said brothers, not son. It's hopeless," Dantiel weeps, his hope and confidence quickly fading from existence.

They wait for any sign from their guardian, Zer Raphael, who said he'll watch over them during their quest to save the world, but none comes. They sit on the rocks, unwilling to leave, for the moment they do, it is their first steps as only a duo of siblings.

"Baelac, didn't we all get magic to help us survive falls? How do we know Ayton doesn't still have it? He could be alive! We have to go after him! If we don't, he could be captured or killed or tortured by some insane beast we know nothing about! Don't you want to do something good today? Then help me help us! Help me get our brother back!" Dantiel shouts. His shallow confidence echoes through his raspy voice, tired from crying so much. Baelac is too shocked to cry. He cannot believe something so terrible can happen so soon.

"You said we should use magic to detect like magic, right?" Baelac reminds Dantiel lovingly.

"Yeah, I did. Help me with it!" Dantiel replies.

The two brothers feel their pockets to ensure they have their fall-resistant talisman and link arms and elbows tightly with fervent determination to reunite with their brother. In linking arms and activating the same spell, beacons of light both red and green shoot up into the dead sky. A pulse of their red and green magic engulfs the black lands and searches for a magical ping response, anything that will tell them their brother is alive. Miraculously, a ping comes back; the smallest sliver of blue light among their red and green dimly shows through, so faint it is almost invisible.

"There he is! Come on, let's go now!" Dantiel and Baelac leap off the cliffside, and they put all of their hope, which isn't much and shrinking by the minute, in their enchantment to survive another great fall. Before they fully jump, however, Baelac hesitates.

"Wait! What if it's a trick? What if we go down there and we find out he's dead and that sliver of blue light we saw was an enemy waiting to kill us?"

"What are you saying? That you don't want to find your other brother? What if it was you down there? Would you be okay if we just completely ignored you and left you somewhere? No, I bet not! Now shut up and jump with me, man!" Dantiel is angry now. What is Baelac's motivation for not doing this?

"I'm just saying I don't trust this. It doesn't feel right to me! We have to protect ourselves, or none of us are gonna survive day 2 here! Okay? So just be smart for once," Baelac huffs back.

"For once? Who are you calling stupid?" Dantiel retorts.

"Hey, I'm just saying the two of you babies immediately collapsed and cried for mommy, and I had to come save both your butts. I can't keep babysitting if we have a whole world to save. Grow the hell up and stop whining! He's gone! And no amount of adventure is gonna bring him back! You jump down there after him., that's on you. I'm out! This is so stupid, you're gonna die if you go down there, I'm telling you now. I'm not fighting you. I'm trying to protect you from yourself."

"Why is it so wrong to want to find your brother? What is wrong with you? You self-absorbed, arrogant gas bag! You only care about yourself and getting some kind of accolade for saving the world," Dantiel mocks.

"That's not what I said. You just need a little help with—" Baelac is cut off.

"YOU JUST NEED A LITTLE PUSH! LEAVE ME ALONE!" Dantiel, in his anger, shoves Baelac, who then stumbles backward and trips off the mountainside as well.

\*\*\*\*\*

"Dantiel, wake up!" Ayton and Baelac yell. Their brother will not budge for the longest time until finally he comes to.

"What, what happened? Ayton! You're alive! You're back!" Ayton is confused by this. "Why are you both looking at me like that?"

Ayton and Baelac smile at each other, crack their necks, and transform into hellhounds, devouring their confused brother like a pack of starving wolves.

\*\*\*\*\*

Have you ever been so distrustful that you can't or indeed shan't trust the very world in which you live? From the bigger picture, aspects like friends and family, to the little things like locations of favorite spots and the very trees you admire? Probably not, but that is precisely what the three brothers are experiencing. While they think that Baelac is angrily shoved off a cliff and that Ayton and Baelac have devoured Dantiel, none of this took place. In fact, nothing has actually happened apart from landing in the dead Arkanya and Baelac needing to save his brothers from various challenges. While he is successful in saving them, and they have finally left the banks of Lake Souviens, nothing else has occurred. What did occur is that the Hell Rose has entrapped Baelac and Dantiel giving them both continuous nightmares, different versions of emotional and mental torture to stop them from their mission. Ayton has indeed fallen, and it is not known what becomes of him since then. Time continues to tick, and with every subsequent tock, the brothers experience some new, twisted, false day. If they can't defeat the Hell Rose, they'll never get out. If they can't defeat the Hell Rose before six days pass, they will become additional roses and are doomed to rot in the meadow forever as another cursed, fiery flower. Two days have passed; only four remain. Ayton is missing and Baelac and Dantiel lie unconscious, trapped by the Hell Rose. As the false day count continues, the bright-orange leaves glow and smoke with celebratory malice, and their bright-red thorns pierce their flesh to further inject the pain the flowers believe they deserve.

Ayton falls farther and farther off the mountain, and he can hear his siblings' cries for him getting faint as he descends through the air, still holding the Hell Rose. In his blackened hand, it transforms into its true form—the black-orange-and-red-colored rose from the cursed meadows. Ayton still has the enchanted talisman to survive a fall from any height, so he plucks petals off the rose one by one, killing the bastard as he falls. The monstrous beast is more animal than plant, and it whines and screams as it dies in his hands. The black in his hand fades as it heals, and the fangs in his mouth shrink back down to normal. His cursed curiosity saves his arse from further poison. With an explosive thud, Ayton makes impact with the ground and body-slams the dead flower. When he brushes off his robes, he stands up and looks at the flower and aims a single hand toward it and shoots boiling water as hard as a fire hose, disintegrating the monster for good. Panting and blooded and sweaty, Ayton wipes his forehead and sighs with relief. As he catches his breath, he looks up, shielding his vision from the sun and wonders how he'll get back to his brothers. He hears something out ahead, but there doesn't appear to be anything. Ayton summons his magic, his eyes glowing brightly, ready to strike if needed.

"Who's there? Show yourself," Ayton beckons.

"You should know by now, my boy!" replies a familiar voice. None other than Zer Raphael approaches from the shadows in the rocky rubble.

"Stop! Prove to me you are who you say, or I will strike you," Ayton threatens. He is not a fool.

"Smart! Tell me, what is the status of the Propheta Fior?" asks the man claiming to be Raphael.

"Well, I gave it to Baelac, but after we told the survivors of Arkanya, it disintegrated when we accepted our destiny." Ayton smiles, knowing that only Raphael will know that since it took place in a corner of the land magicked by a tool that can't be detected by Kalypto. With his realization, he runs over to hug his father figure. Raphael laughs and hugs him back.

"So much has happened, and it's been so misguided so far," Ayton replies.

"Yes, misguided, yes, but what would you say if I were to say to you that only twelve hours had passed since we departed from Earth?" asks Raphael.

"What? How?"

"The stars, my lad, the stars are maps! And some of those maps are chronometers if you know how to read them. According to them and my magic, it has only been twelve hours, but to you, you think it's been days, if not weeks, yes?" Ayton nods and Raphael strikes him across his face. "Snap out if it! You've been under the influence of Yamirzen magic. What did I tell you before you jumped? Never trust anything here! Speaking of which, where are your brothers?" asks Raphael.

"They're up there. I fell off the mountain because I was entranced by that demon rose thing. It tried to kill me. It lured me in and told me to jump and gave me no choice I couldn't control my own body, my own mind."

"It does more than that Ayton. Grab my arm, quick!" Raphael waits for Ayton to link elbows, and he claps his hands together above his head, departing in a flash of lightning and reappearing in the hell rose meadow. "Do not breathe yet. Hold it!" Raphael creates a beautiful, ornate, magical mask for Ayton; it only covers his eyes and nose and is in multiple shades of blue with gold and emerald accents. The swirling design is the identical pattern of Ayton's special magic, and the shade of blue is identical to that of his magic as well. With no tie, the mask makes a perfect seal and also provides Ayton with night vision and other abilities.

"Whoa!" Ayton smiles childishly.

"Come on, we have to save your brothers! If they don't wake up, they'll either die or become one of these cursed roses!"

"What do we do? Nothing I try is working. It's like the flowers have a magic-dampening spell laced within their roots."

"It's up to you. I can do nothing. What are you going to do? Think now! What are the facts of these roses?"

"Well, they feed on fears, they don't require water, and..." Ayton lands on the same page as Raphael.

"That's it! They don't need water! Use your spell to wash them all away!" Raphael levitates to avoid becoming collateral damage and dons his own brown-and-white mask, equally ornate and efficient.

Ayton uses both hands to conjure streams of boiling and freezing water simultaneously and obliterates the monstrous roses once and for all. Their screams truthfully indicate their deaths and release their hold on Baelac and Dantiel. As the magical, frosty water washes over the land, in this one spot, beautiful green grass shows through the black soot and ash.

"Look! You're doing it!" Raphael says. Slowly the sun pierces through the thick fog and shines a cone of daylight on them just for a moment before the day returns to its stormy gray. The two brothers cough and choke as they wake up gasping for clean air, expelling the toxins given by the cursed roses.

Ayton explains what the roses have done and how he survived and tells them to create their own mask to prevent dealing with any of this moving forward. There is no guarantee it will work with every challenge but is better than being without. Or so they think.

Day three of the cursed roses ends; only three remain.

# 24

## The Stars

Half of the time allotted to the three heroes to be alive while under the vexing and entrapping spells of the cursed flowers have gone up, with only three days remaining. They need to do something quick, or else they'll either be murdered within the Yamirzen-filled dreams or be turned into another cursed flower themselves. But how in the world, how in any world actually, can one have a change of heart while that same heart is under the influence of dark magic? At this point, the brothers have absolutely no idea about the difference between cursed life and real life. If they spend one more full day in the flower's circle of power, their own magic will grow attached to that of the flower, and they'll never be able to overcome the illusion.

*****

Zer Raphael, back on Earth far above their heads, paces swiftly back and forth, his shimmering tan-and-green robes flowing around him like a solidified shadow. He holds his head in his hands, rubs his neck, and lets them fall as he toils his mind around how he can help them from here. He no longer has any more of the magical root that allows one to survive great falls, so what is he to do from here?

"Zer Raphael, come quick. Something is attacking us. We need help!" cries a villager.

"What? What is it? What's here now? Who could possibly have gotten here?" replies Raphael. He sets aside his thoughts about his pupils and grabs a twisted, knotted old staff from the wall, and it shines bright green the moment he touches it.

"I"—he swallows—"I think it's one of the skeletons that burned our homes." The villager is visually terrified, traumatically so, as sweat drips from his face as he says this aloud. Raphael steps outside, but it is no ordinary Skrall Army member. No.

It is the highest-ranking member of the Skrall Army, the general commander aka Mauleiter Hollefolter. Robed in what can only be assumed to be magically manipulated tar, the thick, black muck takes the form of a hooded robe but drips, oozes, hisses, and bubbles like a great and dismal swamp. Underneath the robes is something far worse. A half-skeleton half-rotten man. The flesh in small spots is black; other areas are smeared with dried blood, bruises, gashes. The bones are also blackened and somehow polished like smoked chrome. He looks like a robot almost, with the metallic tone and inorganic way he floats so close to the ground as if he is walking, but he isn't. Villagers scream as Mauleiter Hollefolter lifts but a pinky ever so slightly and entire homes and camps erupt in fiery explosions. The shock waves expel citizens over the edge and far down below to their deaths. Hollefolter speaks only the same word on repeat: *Raphael*.

Women scream in the background as the remnants of their torn-apart family are bombarded and burned away. Hollefolter is careful to leave only a handful of survivors, hoping that he'll annihilate all but one from each family so they'll live with nothing but depression and trauma.

Raphael slams his staff deep into the earth and weeps as he sees inadvertently the mounting corpses, magically frozen in their last moments of terror and attempts to form a barrier spell to stop the horror. To everyone's surprise, it immediately works. Zer Raphael's eyes lights bright green with his magic and his anger. The moon reflects off the streaks of tears down his cheeks, looking like a tattoo. Raphael uses his magic to levitate so he can speak to the demon eye to eye and holds his staff toward the thing's throat from outside his barrier.

"What is your purpose here, demon? Have you so little magic that you feel the need to assert yourself against a camp of wounded and sick people? You're disgusting and pathetic." Raphael uses magic to bring pain to the beast. He instantly wishes he hasn't begun conversation. The demon can only speak whatever Kalypto has ordered him to say, which in this case is nothing but simply "Raphael" but now in an ear-shattering screech, one that cracks the earth and crumbles parts of it off tumbling down to Arkanya. Raphael is close to Yidnar back in the day and, therefore, knows more than most about how Kalypto operates his military.

"You can only say 'Raphael.' Well, if it's me you want, then take me but spare my people! They have done nothing and deserve none of your attention. Take me instead." Raphael is hoping that the demon will take him to Arkanya so that he will not even have to use magic and return to his boys.

With a snap of his shiny claw, Hollefolter disarms the barrier and laughs.

"Did you think I obey commands from a tyrant who never shows his putrid face? No, dear boy. I WANTED YOU DEAD! You think you know me and my troops so well. You know *nothing*! You know nothing of torment or pain, but don't worry, it's time to learn a lesson, and I'm here to teach!" Hollefolter screams, holding his hands out before him, conjuring fire that rages between them, ready to burst. Raphael too arms but one hand, holding his staff high to the sky, letting lightning strike his raised staff, ready to throw a bolt at the beast.

Villagers watch this great buildup of magic in awe. Light from the fire and the lightning bathe the remnant of Arkanya, and survivors take shelter, fearing the worst.

At the same time, both Raphael and Hollefolter fire their spells at one another. With a great flash and massive explosion of magic, the two foes strike critical hits at one another, Raphael's bolt of lightning mightily and righteously striking the beast's chest, and Hollefolter's fire erupting from his hands like a portable volcano over Raphael. Slowly the light fades, the sounds trail off to the distance, and the two soldiers lie motionless on the ground. The villagers are hopeful that Raphael is faking his death to fool his opponent. "He's our last hope right now," says some hiding survivors.

"And our only defense from things like this," another survivor piggybacks on the former's point. They nod and weep and continue to watch. For an eternity it seems, neither of them moves an inch.

"I have to go inspect them," one brave woman finally states.

"What? Are you mad? If either of them is alive, you'll be killed from them being startled! Do not go over there, I'm telling you!" the woman's friend urges against this plan heavily. However, the first woman is stubborn and wants to be useful, so she creeps out from behind the boulder and tiptoes toward the demon first. Her friend is worried sick but ready to help and looks around her for anything to use as a backup weapon shall the need arises. She picks up a sharp rock and hopes it won't come to a fight. She'll surely lose.

Ever closer does the friend approach the moonlit alley where the epic but short battle occurred. Suddenly, her foot kicks a stone, and it rolls over and over stopping in the moonlight. It is quiet, but it is the only noise penetrating the air. She, out of fear, turns her back to the demon and changes her mind, wanting to inspect Raphael first. Her friend panics hysterically and muffles her own mouth with her hands as her scared self screams. Hollefolter has unbroken his bones and bends in the most unnatural way and stands back up, uncurling like a snap together doll. Focused on reaching Raphael quietly, the brave woman does not notice this. Hollefolter, without even facing the friend, points an arm at her, and she explodes into a thousand pieces. The woman hears this and whips her head toward where her friend once was but now is replaced by bloodstains on the rocks. She screams and starts running, but the beast too begins running like a hellhound. It crawls and races on all fours, growling and screaming at her. The woman races all around the campsite, careful to try to lose him by going in small alleys. With all the commotion, Raphael wakes up to find his staff has been broken in the duel.

"Hmm. Odd, that usually works. What in…" Raphael comes to full consciousness and sees the epic chase around him. He gestures with his hands and arms as if he is reaching for an arrow from a quiver, and with a glittering effect around him, they both appear for him. The arrow is yellow as gold, and the quiver is white as milk. He aims at the beast with his magical arrows and shoots three at once. Each arrow travels in a different direction, but all three fatally strike the beast. One pierces through his eye sockets, the second tears through his chest and pins him to a tree, and the final one shoots his head clean off, falling over the edge down to Arkanya. The woman is back where she began this evening, behind the same boulders she originally hid from, holding onto one of them to catch her breath.

"You saved my life," she responds, looking up at him.

"You would have done the same," Raphael replies. He waves his right hand in a horizontal circle, cleaning the blood from her friend off the boulders and making a grave for her. "What was her name?"

"Lavender," replies the woman. At that moment, a large wreath of yellow and purple flowers blooms out of nothing at the base of the now appearing ivory headstone.

"Thank you for that too. She kept me alive this whole time. We were like sisters. During the Jigocrugya, we found each other in the middle of the fires. We had both been orphaned and told each other we'd make it through together as a new family of friends." The woman cries and falls to her knees at the new grave for her longtime friend. Raphael kneels beside her to comfort her.

"You garnered much strength from her friendship and support, I see. Do not be sad for long. She is in a far better place than here. I assure you of that," he replies to her.

"Thank you, thank you so much. You've been so nice, and you literally saved my life from certain death. What's your name, stranger?" In the moonlight, Raphael can tell she originally hailed from Denebia as her skin is dark brown with speckles of shining blue, like sky-blue freckles. She has her long, light-brown hair the color of chocolate braided down her back out of her face and is only a few inches shorter than Raphael. She wears a pure suit of leather armor and has brown iron boots and gauntlets. She has picked off items from corpses in order to continue protecting herself as this war continues.

"My name is Raphael. I am a Knight Praer, former advisor to the late Mage Yidnar at the—"

"Temple of Prophecies, yeah, I know all about him. Well, it's nice to meet a friendly face, and thank you for your help once again. I'm Isajella. You are quite skilled with magic by the way," Isajella replies.

"Oh, that? It's taken me what feels like a hundred years to learn, so thank you! Everything except that damned staff worked well," Raphael jests but truthfully.

"You haven't spent much time here, have you? Magic is unpredictable on Earth. This Palacorn, even before the Jigocrugya, was always a weird hub of, well, almost as if it has its own laws for how magic is used. There's no guarantee a spell you've used for years elsewhere works the same way here. What are you doing here anyway? Aren't you supposed to be fighting Kalypto?" Raphael is surprised to know how much she knows but thankful all the same.

Isajella can see this on his face, and they both laugh. "I read a lot, I used to go to the Temple of Prophecies every week when my mom was at work in the Palace of the Falls, or my dad was out away on training for the High Archon's army. So with both of them gone all the time, books and the magical prophecies became my friends." She laughs. "It's sad, though, because at the time, I felt there were too many people out there in the world. You know, why would anyone out of all of Arkanya choose me to be their friend? Now, I'm alone for the exact opposite reason. There's no one left," she cries looking at her friend's grave.

"Come with me, Isajella. I want to show you something," Raphael speaks, and in a flash, they both disappear. Raphael listens to the brave woman and has concocted a plan. He wants to implore her to keep watch of the camp of survivors while he reunites with Ayton, Baelac, and Dantiel to save them from the dark magic they are still under. The sun is nearing a set on the fourth cursed day for them, and Raphael knows this is a race against time. He explains to Isajella the Propheta Fior, the threat of the Lord of Malice, and the current situation the three brothers finds themselves in.

"How am I supposed to do anything to help? They are under a horrible spell, and it's strong. How can we be of any help?" she asks.

"Because you and I have something they haven't—wisdom. They're not fools. I don't mean that. I simply mean to say that you are a natural-born. The three of them were magically aged because Adonai needed them of the fight to save Arkanya, but we have lived many real years of life. Our existence rooted in the natural and magical is precisely what we need in order for any of this to work. Genadenz can still use magical objects to protect this campground, and I can go down there and wake them all up."

"I think it's really great that you want to go back for them. It sounds like you're their only hope. How will you do that?" Isajella asks.

"I'll need water from the fountain here. It's not magical at all. It's perfect. Fill this bottle with water and pour enough for each of the three boys, just enough to wet their face. They don't have to drink it. Once you do that, they'll be alarmed and want to kill you, so show them this." Raphael hands her an old pocket-sized portrait of the four of them—Raphael and Yidnar with Coragio and Puretia—at the temple.

"Wait, if Arkanya is thousands of miles below, and you said you don't have any more of the magic to help me survive the fall, how will you survive getting down there?"

"You didn't think I'd ever actually run out of something magical, did you? I invented that trinket! So I made some more. It's very simple alchemy really. Just have to get the temperature right. Too cold and you travel back in time, too hot and you, well, that's not important. What is important is I did it correctly. So keep this in your pocket and secure it. If it is not on your person, it will not work. You're going to fall thousands of feet to the surface of Arkanya." Raphael arms himself with melee and long-range weapons (crossbow with enchanted arrows like the ones he fired earlier), provides her knowledge to find her way around the dead world without a compass; and after she suits up and understands the plan, Isajella screams. The headless body of Hollefolter has not been defeated and used the same arrows that severed his own head to stab Raphael through the chest and kill him. Isajella weeps as the man who not only is prepared and ready to save his family but also saved her and likely countless others now lies dead. She is tired of things not working, and so she picks up her non-magical sword and fights the headless beast. What will those three innocents do without any help? They are destined to be the greatest purveyors of magic in the world, but they're also just children. Isajella makes up her mind. She is going to avenge her friend and then meet the brothers. Come hell or high water, she is going to do it.

Isajella slashes at the headless figure of Hollefolter multiple times and tears open his side. He reaches at her with his claws and strikes her face, throwing her a hundred feet away. She spits out blood, wipes her forehead, and stands back up.

"You know this only ends one way." Isajella spits. Then she realizes she is talking to a headless mutation of life and laughs at herself. She climbs a tree stump, raises her hands with the sword, and jumps as high as she can to land an overhead attack, stabbing her sword straight into his neck, pinning him deep into the ground.

"Good, now stay there!" She goes back into Raphael's house and grabs all the things he says he needs to get back to the three brothers—the water jug, the magic to survive the fall, and additional magic arrows for the crossbow. She returns to where the enemy is pinned to the ground and saw that the villagers have grabbed knives, swords, and pitchforks. One man walks over to her and says, "Raphael told us his plans weeks ago. He was waiting for the right person to come along who could take his place when he left. Clearly that person is you. You go on. We'll take care of that beast." They shake hands, and as she walks away, the villagers take down the evil Hollefolter until there is nothing left.

# 25

## The Loss of Innocence

Isajella does as she is told and trusts the wisdom of the late Zer Raphael. As someone who does not have magic, she worries greatly about whether or not the magical totem that he has bestowed upon her will work as it shall once she completes her fall to Arkanya. She remembers just then too what Raphael told her about the end of the fourth day for the three brothers. Shall the sun set with them not waking up, they'll be eternally doomed as a withered new flower in the cursed meadows or will be killed within the dream and so too in reality. She whips her head around to gauge the sun. *It is beginning to transition from afternoon to evening*, she thinks, and she knows she has no time to be wary. It is all up to her to rescue the brothers. She has no idea where in the world they can be but trusts in the one true creator that he'll guide her once she descends into the gloomy, burned world, but how? In what method will he help? Will he, indeed, help at all? There is *much* left to chance, something which Isajella seldom has done, but desperate times call for desperate measures. She swallows her fears and chooses to hold onto trust and the totem as hard as she can. She takes a leap of faith and jumps over the edge of the world.

The air is cold as she falls, and her eyes tear up with the rush of continuous air. *This isn't so bad*, she thinks to herself but realizes she hasn't quite looked down yet and swears to herself she won't. Tossing through the air, though, she occasionally does catch a few glances of the blackened ground. Fog appears to be settling in or some other misty white substance. She holds on tighter to faith and to her trust in Raphael's words, and down further she falls until Arkanya new and old are equidistant to her. All this time she has been falling, she thinks about her life, her past with her family, and the times she wished she had more patience and less anger or irritation. She does not deny that there are times she'd fight with her family but no such times when she has less love for them. Distracted by some old memories, she snaps out of it and notices she is just a hundred feet above the ground. She closes her eyes and holds on tighter to the totem until all go black. There is what feels around the dead world like an explosion, its shock wave emanating from the northwest, near the ruins of the Temple of Prophecies.

Meanwhile, Kalypto, who has set out to do what his minions appears to be incapable of, also sees and senses the thunderous entrance of yet another living soul.

"DAMN THEM FOR ALL ETERNITY!" Kalypto's rage intensifies, and the soil beneath him cracks and ruptures like tiny volcanoes beneath his misty self. The white mist Isajella saw while she fell was not fog but him.

The only thing not tainted by the Jigocrugya is the wind, and sometimes in Arkanya, particularly when so much danger is ever-present, nature tends to give man warnings, messages, only whispers to your ears; but trust me when I tell you it is alive, aware, and active. So when the three heroes begin the evening of their fourth day, the breeze picks up that time, and one can swear it is whispering something to them. Isajella begins to hear the message from the winds as well.

"Run, he is coming. Run, girl, run," it calls, blowing her hair out and picking up speed. She grows agitated trying to brush off her clothes from the dust, kissing the totem Raphael gave her, and she looks up at Earth, winkles, and carries on. Harder the wind blows and more she hears the whispers of guidance. Suddenly, it dawns on her, though annoying as it is to have all her hair blowing in front of her face, it is always to the same direction.

"Is it possible?" She guesses and gambles that the wind is not just beckoning her to leave the area but to head in a particular direction—in which it is blowing, using her hair to point her. She laughs at the impossibility and runs in the southwest direction, running with the wind perfectly at her back as hard as she can. The winds push her hard almost as if she are gliding like a great gazelle through the lands to reach her destination in time.

Time! Isajella checks the level of the sun, much farther it has sunk closer to the horizon. She has even less time to make this work. She beckons out to the winds to gust harder to push her faster and faster until she is running so fast the rest of the world becomes a blur. She is worried and hoping again that her gamble is true. Who knows where she is actually headed? What if it is all wrong? Finally, in the distance, she sees a field as far as the eye can see of what looks like millions of fireballs in the ground. She has in fact reached the burning meadows.

*Oh! Oh my gosh. This is so good! Thank you! Thank you everyone that helped! Ugh, now where do I go? Ugh,* she thinks hard, reviewing everything Raphael said about the boys, that they'll be unconscious, they are separated from the third brother, and that, *oh!* One of them fell off the cliff where the other two remains. The sun is bright orange now at the tail end of the ever poignant fourth day, and she feels tears coming but tells herself forcefully "not yet!"

Again, she runs hard up the hill toward the edge and follows her instinct only. The wind has stopped; she is all alone. This is completely up to her. Time is against her as is Kalypto.

Nearing ever closer, the white thunder clapping and lightning flashing storm of Kalypto's haze is approaching. Slowly, things in the border of the meadow begin to be covered in a thin layer of black ice, ceasing any ability to control itself but still feel everything.

Isajella starts gasping and laughing with relief, finding in the shrinking distance the bodies of two boys. They have lost much blood from the thorned vines of the cursed meadows, and she fights with them with her dagger to set the kids free. She slices herself a few times, and the sun inches closer and closer to the horizon. She can almost feel it touch her skin. She breathes heavily, panicking, wanting to get everyone awake soon. She has sliced and kicked and stomped and sliced some more, chipping away at the blood-covered cages of thorned vines and grabs the non-magical water from the fountain of Earth to wet their faces. She waits for a half second, and they don't move.

"Come on! Wake up! We don't have much time! Wake up!" she yells and slaps their faces. Finally, they start moving and slowly open their eyes just as the sun has touched the horizon.

"Oh, thank the creator! Now come with me over the cliff! We need to save your brother before it's too late!"

"Wait, how, who?" Dantiel is disoriented and confused and thinking she is another illusion meant to harm them but has absolutely no energy to fight physically. Verbally, he protests like a grumbling progressivist. Isajella grabs him by the shoulder and links arms with the two of them who squirms and protests, but she shows them the photograph of Raphael and Yidnar, and they pass out in disbelief.

"Oh, for crying out loud," she moans. To survive jumping this cliff, she has to hold the magical item in her mouth and hold onto two boys tightly. She holds both of their hands, and so all their arms are linked together firmly. She can see Kalypto's crown piercing through the storming, quaking haze in the approaching view but waves goodbye as she jumps over the edge down again to the lower level. Just as she has begun falling, Kalypto has reached out far with his six-fingered claw and attempts to slice her throat, screaming with his failure. He screams and roars with rage, his voice breaking and crumbling mountaintops.

Isajella reaches the bottom and wakes up the other two brothers. She can't see the sun as she is behind rocks but doesn't care anymore. She tries with all her might to wake Ayton, but even after dousing all the water on him from the bottle, he refuses to budge. The two brothers cry and creep around the corner of the boulder to see the sun and see that it only has a few inches above the horizon. The brothers weep, worried they have lost their firstborn brother so soon. Isajella is determined to bring him out of the hell he surely faces and holds him in her arms.

"It's not your time to die. You need to wake up. I did it. I brought you the water," she cries. The brothers' eyes are as wide as dinner plates.

"Water? Give it here quick!" Baelac says. He grabs the bottle and sees there is but half a drop left in the bottle. He opens the cork and holds it above Ayton's palm. "Come on, work!" he shouts.

Isajella grabs Dantiel and walks over to the edge of the boulders. They can't hear Kalypto screaming anymore, which worries them. They both arm their weapons and stand their ground as Kalypto descends gently down to the lower level with them. He is about a hundred yards away when the black ice creeps and slithers its way through the blackened and dead soil toward Ayton.

Half a second before the ice reaches Ayton, the drop of water falls out of the bottle as Baelac holds his breath to ensure nothing will make this go wrong. It falls and splatters a tiny pool into his hand, which immediately pulses light, bright blue, and Ayton's eyes immediately open, sending two beacons of blue light high into the twilight sky. With just a sliver of the sun left, the brothers have all awoken just in the nick of time. Any slower and they'll all be dead. At the same time, though, only Ayton is untouched by the black ice. Isajella, Dantiel, and Baelac are as solid but living statues. Kalypto grins with his vermillion-red fire behind his skull and in his jaw. He clanks his bony fingers together, which sounds like wooden wind chimes in the summer, and lets out a chuckle.

"So I murder your parents, and now you come to do me the honor of dismantling your hope. How poetic!" Kalypto taunts. The white mist of his stormy self then engulfs them, and his brothers cannot see anything but Ayton's blue light from his magic.

"You did nothing. It was Massacara who killed them," replies Ayton, laughing at the smugness and misplaced pride of Kalypto.

"AND WHO DO YOU THINK COMMANDED HER?" Kalypto has pinned Ayton to the ground with the chin bone of his skull. "No matter. You are here now. That's what counts. Tell me, dear child, what is the happiest memory you have?" Kalypto calmly asks. The red fire turns to a soft pink, and Kalypto begins drooling from his mouth. Ayton finds himself incapable of doing anything but think through all his happy memories. They aren't much admittedly, but they are warm and strong.

"Aw, so sweet. That was awful nice of your brothers to care for you and protect you. Hold onto that feeling, little boy, for love is..." Cracks appear through Kalypto's skull. "Love is an illusion. It feels real now. At the start, it always does, but allow me to show you the truth!" Kalypto digs his claw deep into the back of Ayton and tries to cleave his soul as he has done so many other times, only this time something is different. Suddenly, Adonai appears again from the skies in beautiful purple, turquoise, and yellow clouds. He is furious with Kalypto's disobedience.

"Remember our agreement, demon! You have no power on this day! Be gone or suffer the consequences of your feeble, dusty mind! Away with you!" Adonai reminds and explains that only on the anniversary of the birth of the heroes does Kalypto have no power to harm them, and that is today.

"Unfortunately, today is only minutes away from ending, and tomorrow you'll be at his mercy again. Remember this well! Each fifteenth of Idamay, you are safe from harm from sunrise to sunset. But know this. Something stopped him before I came upon you all tonight, and it wasn't me. Whatever it was is within you, my son," Adonai speaks and gives chills of joy and hope to the four of them. Isajella is moved beyond words at his sight and falls to her knees with delight and overwhelming happiness. Adonai vanishes as quickly as he came, and Isajella passes out with so much going on. Ayton hugs his brothers and disarms his blue magic. They have survived impossible challenges by the skin of their teeth and not alone.

"You, see? We're gonna get through this, all of us," Ayton says, smiling with tears rolling down his cheek.

# 26

## The Plan

Isajella, for the next few days, has to consistently prove she is indeed *not* a trick provided by the new Arkanya and that she can be trusted. The brothers absolutely do not trust their own sensations, thoughts, or eyes, having just barely survived the ordeal with the cursed flowers. While weeks and a whole month have passed according to their perceptions and experiences with other beasts and Yamirzen magic thus far, only an actual week has passed since they fell to this plane. The quadruple set of unwilling companions venture from the pit beneath the cursed meadow hills to somewhere more condensed to not be out in the open area. The jackal moon bears the face of a skull still, much to the continued dismay of the troupe, and on they walk through the night. There are no charming sounds of nighttime life—no crickets, no dragonflies, no birds, nor woodland animals. Everything is dead, and the lands they trudge through are black as pitch. The air grows colder, and Isajella holds her arms, attempting to use her body heat as a cloak.

"Here, Isajella, take mine," Ayton offers her his robes. His tunic and armor keep him comfortable enough and, even without, wants to make sure the only lady present is taken care of. Their hands inadvertently touch when he offers his robe, and she accepts while shivering. *His warm hand feels nice*, she thinks, but just moments ago she is yelling at him. She is caught completely off guard and tells herself to say something snarky to mask the newfound spark between them.

"I don't need your charity, but thank you," she barks, blushing. Ayton, being a male, is completely clueless. Baelac, on the other hand, watches from the back as this unfolded. Suddenly, she feels a mild sting in her palm. "Ow!" she shouts.

"I'm sorry! I guess I still had some magic armed." He cups his hands together, and the blue light disappears. The literal spark between them is seen by all. Dantiel glares as he still absolutely does not trust this girl, and Baelac laughs. It is unclear if it is a laugh to say, "you got to be kidding me," or a laugh as in, "good for him." Regardless, it makes a tense situation much more so.

"You only survived because I came back for you all! Of anything in this entire world, I am the only thing you can be sure of! I thought you'd be relieved to have someone you can rely on!" Isajella is frustrated and tired of being interrogated at every opportunity.

"Why did you come back? Who even are you? Why do we matter to you at all? We don't even know you! What do you want from us?" Dantiel exclaims. Baelac agrees with his skeptical sentiment.

"Yea, why do you care? We've never even met before. How could we?" asks Baelac.

"Until recently, I had no idea who you were or about the Propheta Fior, or any of it. But up above, back on Earth, we were attacked by some beast, another general in Kalypto's army probably left behind from when that corner of the land was severed from the rest of Arkanya. Anyway, we were attacked, and for some reason, it focused a lot of its attacks on me and..." she cries, thinking about her sister. "Me and my late sister, but I was saved by Raphael. He sacrificed himself so that I could have a chance to carry on what he started—to make sure you three are successful because this torment and death are never going to stop until Kalypto is defeated! It's actually worse than death. Everyone he kills is prevented from resting in peace. He eats their souls. It's as though spiritually they never existed at all. I lost my sister. This involves me too. I am in whether you want me to be or not. And I am tired of being mistrusted when none of you would even be alive had I not met Raphael. How would I know any of this if I was lying? We are also wasting time we do not have. Kalypto failed. Do you think he's going to patiently wait to strike again? We need a plan." Isajella gauges the temperature of the room and can tell, at her delight, she finally gets through to the three of them. She is absolutely right too; time is ticking, and Kalypto has to be dealt with.

"If you'll pardon us for not curtsying. While we no longer believe you're a trick, it remains to be seen if you actually want us to succeed in defeating the Lord of Malice. So for now, just don't get in our way. I can't speak for any of them, but if you do, I will stop you myself. Is that clear?" asks Baelac. He is very protective of the only family he has left.

"Okay, so how in the blazes are we going to defeat Kalypto? We certainly can't use magic. Look what he's been capable of," Dantiel says.

"No, you're right. We shouldn't attack with magic, but we can stall him with it. We'll create a system of magical barriers to stall him from getting to us, to buy us as much time as we can. We should also think about powerful non-magical weapons and tools. Any thoughts?" All of them sit silently for a moment, and then Ayton's mind lights up, figuratively.

"Wait. Oh my gosh, I've got it! The Jigocrugya was a magical reversal, right? It's not the end of the world. We still have hundreds of people on Earth right, Isajella?" he asks, pacing the floor with his excitement.

"Yes," she replies, confused as to where his mind is taking him.

"And who are we, brother?" Baelac asks.

"We are the descendants of the Drakulogons. We are the prophesied heroes, the true victors of Arkanya. We have to believe in ourselves because Isajella is right, there aren't any magical, legendary items to go find or sages to learn from. Everyone is dead! The whole world has been turned on its head—the very nature is poisoned against us. So let's go out there and show Kalypto what he brought upon himself. Let's take the fight to him tonight!" exclaims Ayton.

Just as the youngest of the three heroes has united and realigned their mission upon their return to Arkanya, the ground begins to shake violently. Thunder rumbles in the distance over the hills, and the thick, black clouds sink heavy with a storm coming. Lightning flashes in red-and-yellow-like fire, and it begins to rain. Each raindrop is alive and vile. The water droplets don't splatter like normal raindrops; they are armed with Yamirzen magic, and each one is a different type of torment magic intended to bring pain upon contact. The tree stumps from the dead forest nearby wilt further as the rain hinders their remaining mediocre existence. Where in a land that has not been touched by the horrors of toxic and lethal magic of Yamirzen, rain gives life. Arkanya's rain intends to take life away. As the rain falls, it coats the world in additional thick, black-and-brown muck. This rain is more like oil, and as each drop lands, the droplet remains in bulbous form and burrows like a beetle into whatever it has landed on—rotting corpse, dead plant life, and so forth. Once it burrows, it turns the full body of whatever it is completely black and emits the smell of rotten eggs, the smell of a recently burned-out candle, the smell of sulfur. The Yamirzen rain hisses and sizzles as it coats the world in blackness and in the smell of death. Kalypto gazes out across the lands, watching the red-and-orange lightning bathe the world in his favorite shade of foul.

With the eerie backdrop of quiet but steady life-quenching rain and flashes of red lightning, the quartet of odd young adults huddle together, trying to figure out how to defeat the chief of all darkness.

Isajella meekly proposes that the heroes attempt bringing happiness to Kalypto, redeeming him so that he no longer wishes to do ill will and undo the terror that he has brought to the world. The problem with this plan though is twofold: 1) The likelihood there is enough humanity left inside him to listen and want to change is less than 1 percent, as just by looking at him, one can see he is no longer human. He mocks humanity with his mere existence, a physical form that is reminiscent at best of humanity. 2) The likelihood any of the four of them can survive long enough to tell a sob story that he'll pay attention to is also zilch.

"Isajella, that's like saying "Why don't we just ask the devil to stop being a bad guy? Grow up, okay. We need an actual plan." Baelac's patience for plans or things that won't work grows thin.

"Hey, easy, brother. I know we're all at our wits' end, but we can't be rude. Isajella, he does have a point, though. If there was a way we could change him, that would be great, but look what it's done. There's no reasoning with that," Ayton concludes.

Baelac has an idea, but it is a huge risk. "What if we reunite Earth with the rest of Arkanya? That way our numbers go from three to half a thousand. We could give everyone a drop of the potion of Nauz because now, with the Jigocrugya reversing, everything magical potion that used to take away magic gives it! We could raze a magical army and storm him in a battle." Baelac starts off to a good start.

"And then what? We'll beat him to death? He's already dead! What's your other option? We magic him to death? In case you haven't noticed, if we could defeat him with magic, we obviously would have by now," replies Isajella.

"Would we though? Think about it for a moment. We landed here about a week ago now, and the minute we come back home, we sprout wings like magical birds and soar in the sky without even trying. Raphael told us no one in Arkanya could ever fly without some sort of magical item. All we had was ourselves! If we can do that without even trying, think about what we could do if we did try! Then multiply that by three. I'm telling you, all we need is right here inside of us. We don't need any legendary, special, hard-to-find item. We don't need some old sage. We don't need anything but ourselves, and we have to believe in ourselves." Ayton is on a soapbox as he notices everyone is looking at him profoundly and poignantly. His speech, though unexpected, is absolutely true, for the three boys are indeed everything they need. In fact, they could have achieved this and so much more were it not for the simple fact that they still are not completely sold on the belief that the Propheta Fior is about them specifically. Almost on cue, the two remaining brothers shake their heads and frown.

"You can't do that. *We* can't do that," Baelac rebuts.

"He's right," Dantiel agrees.

Isajella senses a family feud coming and remains silent, but this time does hold Ayton's hand, surprising both of them.

"Why? Why can't we do this?" he asks.

Isajella winces.

"Because you can't throw away your life based on some fairy tale! It's not true!" Baelac says, yelling and stopping all of them from walking further.

"Ayton, he's right. You have to listen to him. It took us basically the whole time we've been back here to be all three united, plus the actions of a fourth party! We can't throw our lives away for something ten times less certain," Dantiel tries to rationalize away his brother's belief.

"Yidnar believed in us! We owe it to him to try it my way!" Ayton feels passionate about this now. He can tell he strikes a chord with his brothers but maybe not enough.

"Yea? Look where that got him. I can't lose you too. You're all I have left of our family. Everyone we love, everyone who believes in that fairy tale is dead," Dantiel speaks, weeping, thinking of their innocent and loving mother and father.

"They weren't just killed; they had their very souls ripped and torn away from their body and then eaten by a grotesque, cursed monster. I can't lose you to that," Baelac finishes.

"I love you, brother, but we have to try! We can't do nothing, and any other plan is not going to be strong enough. We are the *only* thing that can stop him and put an end to this horrendous darkness. I know you don't want to lose me, and I don't want to lose you either, but death is just a part of life, one that everyone has to take. It doesn't have to be this bad, horrible thing to avoid. Death, though terribly sad because they're gone, can also be beautiful. Had our parents not put up a fight, we wouldn't be here. They died to make sure we were alive so that we could enact that prophecy. That's it. That's the only reason we are alive. Well, that and Yidnar saved our asses when we were barely a day old, but seriously, we owe it to Yidnar for his sacrifice for us. We owe it to our parents for their sacrifice, and if none of that is enough for you, you owe it to yourself, if you just have faith in the creator that he gave us all a task we must accomplish, that he gave us a task only we could do. If you don't believe that, you've lost yourself," Ayton explains.

Dantiel collapses, the proverbial and emotional weight of all that Ayton just spoke is too much at once, and he faints. He is healthy and okay, but he faints.

Baelac weeps, worried this all will only end one way, one or more of his brothers will die. He suddenly hears a raspy and cold voice in his head. "Just one will die?" And then it chuckles and falls silent.

The quartet of heroes are protected by Ayton's magic as his right hand shines bright teal-blue, and his magic generates a shield around each of them, parting the falling Yamirzen rain like a mother parts her son's hair to comb it. The hissing grows louder and more vigorous as the bewitched rain attempts and fails to resist Ayton's magic, hissing like a thousand snakes all around them. When Dantiel comes to, the rain has intensified as has the lightning. Isajella has made camp while everyone is bickering and discussing, and Ayton uses his magic to try to cloak and make them all invisible as they sleep. As hard as he tries though, there is one who can still see them and grows repulsed and furious with their continued existence. Kalypto travels undetected by the sleeping heroes and, with one echoing chuckle, lightly taps a cursed claw on the heart of Baelac, turning the skin on his chest as black as tar. As silently as a leaf flapping on a branch in a slight breeze, Kalypto has come and gone while vanquishing Baelac's strongest attribute: his mercy.

# 27

## Deception

When the next morning comes, the sun illuminates not just the lands but the gravitas of the situation. Aside from the increasingly abysmal fact that they are still on the decayed version of Arkanya, they are also down a member of the band, and finger-pointing has begun.

One of the things about the new Arkanya we have mentioned before, is that the longer one spends in the misty lime-green-hued Yamirzen fog, the more one's loyalties are changed. That aspect has not been experienced by the heroes…that is, not until now.

To say that Isajella is under the gun, or should I say under the wand, is a gross understatement. She has not been trusted this entire time, but now one of the brothers is missing, and it's scarce to think of another more egregiously accused person.

"And nothing bad happened to any of us until you miraculously showed up one day. Yeah, uh-huh. Tell me, Isajella, how did someone or something take my brother and yet not happen to wake any of us up? Who's the only one here who disappears or reappears or does anything like this before?" Baelac's eyes are a dingy lime green under the heavy influence of the Yamirzen fog.

"Oh, go ahead and blame me again. Take the easy route instead of facing the fact that you are to blame! You never pay them any attention and then scratch your head wondering where one of them runs off to! If you spent more time with your family and less time channeling your magic, maybe this wouldn't have happened!" Baelac waives a hand as if trying to dismiss himself from the petty argument like a child will swat away an annoying bee. However, Isajella defends herself, though, equally under the influence of the venomous fog.

"And another thing! If I hadn't disappeared and suddenly came back, *all* of you would be dead! Am I right? That's more than you've ever done! Do you even love your family? Or are they just pawns in your belief of that stupid prophecy?" Isajella is proud of the things she gets off her chest and exhales a sigh of relief but quickly draws it all back in, gasping at the hideous sight of an angry Baelac charging at her with his strong hands. Baelac turns his head instantly when she finishes her speech and holds her throat in his hands.

"Don't you ever say something like that again. Everything I do is for my family. You got that? Or do you not even know what family is? What am I saying? Of course, you don't." Isajella slaps him with her fist, sending him to the ground and releasing his grip on her. Isajella has now pinned Baelac to the ground under her foot, stepping on his ankles causing him to yell in pain.

"You are not gonna say another snide thing about me, or if you do, I'll break your ankles and leave you here to be ripped apart by some new twisted beast in this cursed and wretched world. Need I remind you we aren't alone here, so while I am battling your precious, damaged ego, Kalypto is out there *with your brother*, just waiting to pounce! Or worse, kill him and come after us next!" Isajella hisses.

Baelac controls a tree branch to smack her away from him, sending her flying through the air a hundred feet away. The two has blooded each other badly thus far. Neither of them can fight the curse urging them to hurt the other, and nothing can they feel but the other one's pain. Though they can't resist the twisted curse, they are conscious of it. This is Kalypto's way of breaking people, people with good hearts. For you see, it isn't just a fight among brothers that makes this dark; siblings fight all the time. What makes this dark is the fact that the three brothers Ayton, Baelac, and Dantiel only have each other. They made new friends along the journey, but as far as their blood line is concerned, they are it. So to have two of them fight so violently is unnerving and scary for Ayton. He loves his family and can't bear to endure the very person he loves push him away in order to tear himself apart. He tries from the sidelines to use as much magic as he can to stop them, to help them see what he sees, that they are family and that shall matter above all else. His magic is folly, sparking off as if hitting an invisible wall put up by the brother's new preference of hate over love, strife and drama over peace.

Ayton cries as he tries a thousand different charms, watching them go totally unnoticed a thousand times. Isajella holds his shoulders and urges him to stop.

"Ayton, stop! It's not working, don't you see? They don't want to be helped. They're under the Yamirzen fog. They believe they are justified and right. You can't help them," she cries to him. She loves him and hates to see him get hurt too. She also believes it is wrong to try to force people who are not ready to be close and kind. People need space when lines are crossed, space and time to heal and see the other has changed for the good, and that is assuming both parties want a better relationship. Currently, Baelac and Dantiel do in fact want to not be fighting, but the fear and the doubt in their journey and cause replace the love they have for each other. Egos step in the way, feelings are hurt, and blows are struck. Two people who, without any doubt at all, shall never throw punches are grabbing for rocks to hurt the other even more.

"Isajella, they're my brothers. I can't just sit by and watch my family tear itself apart! I'm tired of this! It's bullshit! It's not right! We're a family and need to act like it." He sighs.

"You're right, Ayton. It is complete bullshit, but it's shit they have to resolve on their own. Otherwise, it won't be real. Otherwise, it won't last. You have to be strong and let them handle this. You've tried all you can to step between them, and it's only hurt you, right? So stop, stay with me, and take a breath." Ayton disarms his magic, deluminating his eyes and hands. Suddenly, he senses something, or rather, don't sense something. The Yamirzen fog they all believe is bewitching the minds of his brothers has gone. The lime-green fog has lifted, but still the two slug each other. A single solemn tear rolls down his cold, reddened cheek. He worries the family may not heal from this, that it may change forever somehow.

"Ayton, what is it?" Isajella asks.

"It's gone. The cursed fog has lifted. Why aren't they stopping?" Ayton has turned on his heel to face Isajella. She holds her mouth and points, with tears streaming like small waterfalls down her chocolate face.

Dantiel stands up now charging magic in his hands and defending his home. "This may be a cursed land, but it's not wretched! It's up to us to stop it, and right now that means you! I am constantly two steps behind you in your shadow. Can't I be free of you? I am the hero, not you!" Dantiel's jealousy and insecurity comes out full force as he uses magic to stop his brother and bring him pain and agony. The three of them fight each other intensely, and as time goes on, things begin to escalate, the risk of dying grows more stressful, and the injuries continue to mount. The hatred between Baelac and Dantiel seems more real than the fog should have brought to light, however, and finally, Isajella is left totally alone while Baelac, shrouded in pride and arrogance, slugs it out with his green magic against his brother Dantiel who wallows in self-pity, immaturity, and insecurity. He is insecure about his role in the saving of the world and wants to make sure that he is significant. What he has lost sight of is that he is important as a brother of Baelac and Ayton and another wielder of the Drakulogon magic, blessed by the one true creator and their parents. What he only sees now is that he felt he isn't useful, isn't needed, or isn't wanted around. He feels alone and isolated and uncared for. He is very wrong, of course, but the longer they fight and linger in the cursed, twisted thick, yellow fog, the more they grow to hate the other. Dantiel and Baelac sadly continue fighting, and while Dantiel begins to cry, feeling his own pain he has been burying more and more, Baelac too weeps, realizing he is totally out of control, unable to stop hurting his brother due to the loyalty-changing fog. All he can think to do is hum a song in his head and hope telepathically that his brother can hear it, the very song that Yidnar sang to them as babies at night to go to sleep. Dantiel can indeed hear the somber hymn, and the two feel strong brotherly love but also fear and terror from being unable to stop themselves from fighting due to the fog. Blood is drawn, and wounds are sliced on each other. Baelac has lapsed into a trance and will have no recollection of this fight, but he will remember seeing the life fade from his dearest brother's eyes as the red, blessed magic dims from Dantiel's hands and eyes for the last time as he falls to the ground, pale as snow and hair black as night but with a new white streak from the fear he faces in this fight. The wind changes suddenly, a sign to Isajella that things have indeed changed forever. Baelac is finally free of the toxic fumes thanks to the new winds, but the deed is done, and his brother is gone.

Ayton and Isajella slowly approach the site of his brothers and collapse to their knees, screaming and crying. The absolute worst has happened, but in an even more terrible way than has Kalypto directly killed Dantiel. The ground begins to shake, rumbling and growling as if to express distaste for this twist of fate, reminding the two remaining brothers of the original prophecy that it is up to the three of them to save their home.

It is as if the creator has cupped Baelac's ears with his hands; all sound is muffled, and all vision is tunneled as he slowly realizes what he's done. Baelac weeps, coming to terms with his trauma and holding his dead brother tightly in his arms. He has done what he thinks he never can or will. Granted he is cursed, but to him this is no excuse. There is no forgiveness for murder, no retribution for killing his own family, and no way forward. Baelac doesn't even care if there are other beasts and creatures in the area that aims to kill him. All he cares about is already dead and another one missing. He feels he has utterly and completely failed, turning into what they are supposed to be fighting. Ayton and Baelac hugs each other, with Baelac totally losing his control, and weeping and sobbing, pulling with anger with himself at Ayton's robes, and screaming into his shoulders.

Isajella tries as hard as she can to spread love and tells them all through her own tears of shock, "I know it hurts, but it wasn't you, Baelac. It was Kalypto. He is the one whose magic did this to you and him."

"No, you heard Ayton. It was me! The fog lifted, but I kept going. I kept going and because of me, now he's dead. Because of me." Baelac waves a hand and conjures a beautiful but secluded fortress high in the crown of the forest, wishing to not be seen again.

Suddenly, hundreds of green butterflies swarm to his armor and chip away at it, leaving behind just Baelac's tunic and trousers. A similar swarm of blue butterflies chip away at Ayton's armor. At first, Baelac weeps and weeps, unwilling to move from this position, thinking in his broken state that if he holds onto his brother, he won't be the man who killed his brother, for any steps he takes from this moment, that's the kind of man he sees himself as. He thinks it is his sin of murder that disarms the magical gift from their creyfather Raphael, but how wrong he is. He wishes and hopes that the world will freeze in time with him, but it angers him that it doesn't, that everything carries on. Life continues as scheduled; nothing even slows down. Instead, a blinding light comes down from the heavens, and a warmth enters their wintry forest that they haven't felt in an age. A strangely sweet, feminine voice echoes, saying, "Be kind, have strength, and love always." The spiritual woman holds out her hand and lifts Baelac's chin and kisses his forehead. "Remember your path, my son. Do not stray, or it will be all our undoing. You mourn the loss of your brother, but fear not, for it was not you who slain him but the dark Lord of Malice, Kalypto. Stay true to your path, my son. Be kind, have strength, and love always." And the light and warmth glimmer away.

Isajella watches as the light dims and the spirit returns to the heavens above. Ayton feels his heart flutter when she leaves and smiles, having seen his mother for the second time. Ayton snaps his fingers and waives his right hand in a half circle away from his right ear. He has placed a sound-muting charm over their site. He doesn't want anyone else to hear his plans.

"Isajella, we need to take the fight to Kalypto now. Time is of the essence! And I know what I must do. Our mother gave me the clues, and it's up to Baelac and me to do it. We're gonna bring the fight to Kalypto, but it's not any ordinary fight. We need to get him alone, no armies, no minions, just us three. Any ideas?" asks Ayton. He has a plan *finally*.

"Now we're talking. Well, we still have people on Earth who are willing to fight," Isajella remembers.

"But that's only a handful of survivors."

"Yes, but you have magic. Why don't you cast an illusion spell and make it look to Kalypto as if you have an enormous army of great soldiers? Use them as a distraction so he has to exhaust all his minions on your army, then you ambush from the rear," Isajella suggests. "My dad taught me some things, and I'm a hunter. It's a gift like any other." They both laugh.

"That settles it then! But we need a backup in case he sees our illusion," Ayton explains. "What if we split up Baelac and me in two separate places? That way, if he sees our blunder, we can still attack."

"Oh, do you know some mysterious spell to take out Kalypto we've never heard of?" Isajella asks smartly.

"No, we still need to steal the potion of Nauz. The magical lake is one of the only things unchanged since the Jigocrugya. I bet if we use that, we can reverse the potion and use it to take away Kalypto's magic."

"It's worth a try, it's the only shot we have."

\*\*\*\*\*

Kalypto, meanwhile, instead of rejoicing the death of one of the three saviors, is soaring through the sky like a meteor, only instead of hurling downward, he is rising higher and higher into the air. He remembers that the heroes began all this mess by crashing down to the changed Arkanya, which must mean they came from somewhere high. His logic is correct, although he cannot see anything. For Yidnar's magic, though old, is still true. Using a wand from the tree at the heart of the world means that Kalypto is incapable of seeing anything cast from it. But Kalypto can feel a great something. He transforms into a skull with a black mist and maneuvers through the air like a gross collection of snakes slithering through the sky. With his claws outstretched, he searches for the source of the magical detection he senses, changing course erratically to follow the magic as accurately as he can until finally the feeling is so immense he winces with a bit of displeasure. He grins in his terrible, crowned skull, and the fire within glows magenta and billows out of his mouth and eyes. He charges his massive stonelike claws with as much Yamirzen magic as he needs, glowing them bright red and yellow, and thrust them deep into the magical force field and begins clawing at the shield with a heft and vigor none knew he has. Kalypto laughs at his own power to force open the impenetrable, to break the unbreakable. "There is none greater than I." He laughs. At last, the final piece of the wretched, magical shield from the damned tree is shattered.

"Greetings, my friends." He laughs again. When he looks back down, he only sees a collection of wooden puppets and marionettes scattered around. This is a conjured decoy of brilliant design, good enough to fool the master of deceit himself.

Kalypto has had his fill of the disgusting existence of light and heroes and takes extreme measures. With this foolish misstep, Kalypto is also, for the first time in his horrible existence, feeling weak. But how? He absorbed more souls and took more lives than any other foe in any other world. How can he possibly be getting weaker?

"My lord, are…are you not the least bit concerned about what the three, well, now two heroes are doing? They're a source of light in the darkness you brought upon this world. More than that, they appear to have found love," his servant says.

Kalypto trembles at the uttering of that L word. It is so-called love that brought his mother to loathe his father; it is love that drove his father down a path of twisted self-righteousness to want to amass dark Yamirzen magic to "protect his family," and thus inject his only child with a false life. It is love that ruined his family and drove him to insanity.

"How can they be so cruel? I can think of no harsher sentence than to 'find love.'" Kalypto stares at himself in the reflection of a crystalline formation in the mountainside on the walls of the cave-like lair of his. He sees the fire in him dwindles, down from a roaring wild blaze to a bonfire. He grows more and more hatred for the concept of love and more and more hatred for himself, that his only experiences with love turn out to be nothing but fiction followed by murder and becoming either an orphan or a murderer depending on who tells the tale. Kalypto smashes the crystalline formation and shakes the lair, intensely shaking the ground and startling the scared servant. Kalypto is forged out of the absence of love and is the personification of hatred and malice and bloodlust. It shall have come as no surprise that in the ashes of his destruction of the world, the heroes finding love shall weaken his Yamirzen powers for it means there is a little bit less hatred in Arkanya, a little bit of hope.

"The light is volatile and dangerous, my lord. It could spread like fire or bleed through the shadows. It's unpredictable, and I think they want more of it," says the servant.

"They want light. I'll give them more light than they could ever ask for," he hisses and growls as he storms back down to his lair, exploding through the mountainside of his hellish fortress. His pathetic servants are eager to please him, but he smacks them away killing most of them. He drags their lifeless bodies, tears out their souls, and makes a curse to bewitch the skies to bleed fire.

*Wait! Perhaps I can bring not only light, but also love!* He snaps two claws together, and in a horrific explosion of white fire in the shape of a skull, Isajella vanishes from before Ayton. Kalypto begins storming throughout the lands leading up to his fortress, building terrible mental prisons filled with painful hexes any one of them can impossibly escape. Some will hasten your age, others will continuously transform your shape so you have no control over yourself, while others will force you to imagine false realities, all allowing Kalypto to watch the pathetic heroes be tortured in reality and killed one by one like the hollow puppets they are to him. Kalypto has many powers but only one weakness. He is so evil he can no longer even see goodness. Using his powers to coerce the three brothers into fighting each other to the death and ultimately succeeding in doing so is one of the darkest ways to kill them. By turning their love as a family into the very weapon used to kill, Kalypto is able to bring down a hero with the aid of another. So finding his nemesis is a challenge. In order to bring them to him, he kidnaps Isajella and has terrible plans of his own awaiting the silly heroes.

The wretched heroes are also stronger than he wants to give them credit for, however. Most citizens when met with Kalypto kill themselves upon seeing him. The heroes, however, delivers sassy remarks and do not harm themselves at all, that is, unless exposed to the Yamirzen fog.

"An excellent form of murder, my Lord," grovels a grotesque pairing of a weasel with a lion cub.

"That is nothing compared to what I'll do to them once they're here. Go to the two boys and bring them to me alive. I want nothing to suspect who you are, and I want them to think this is all part of their own plans. Bring them to me, and I shall feast on their vile souls and teach them finally that happiness is a lie, an illusion that must be put aside."

"But, my Lord, if I don't know what their plans are, how can I possibly—" he is cut off.

"Do as I say or be cast into the fiery pits of Yamirzen. Your choice. But remember, you'll never leave Yamirzen!" Kalypto laughs hysterically as the disgusting but helpless minion knows not at all what to do and has no choice. The weasel remembers his family and remembers that Kalypto pinned him to a tree and forced him to watch as he ate his family and then enslaved him forever to his will.

Will, as Kalypto aptly named him, is sent on his way to betray the heroes to their deaths.

# 28

## The End

Ayton, Baelac, and Isajella regroup the following eve to discuss the plans Ayton and Isajella concoct the night prior: to steal the potion of Nauz to eliminate Kalypto's magic, use an illusioned army to lure Kalypto's forces away getting Kalypto alone, and strike from an unexpected direction. It is a long shot and includes many maybes and hopefully, but it is the only plan they have. Mind you, all of this is, of course, discussed in the enchanted, sound-muting shield by Ayton for insurance.

"Right, so we need to stick together and find the potion first. Once we have that, Kalypto will likely be on our tail detecting such additional magic. We need to be ready," Ayton explains.

"Wait, he's the most powerful wielder of Yamirzen magic, right? How do we know he's not listening right now? And yes, I know about your sound shield, but really? You've been doing magic for not even a year, and Kalypto's been dropping jaws for centuries. I'm just saying we need to be careful—" Isajella is cut off.

"Wait, Baelac, what day is it?" Ayton's ears perks.

"Are we really doing this? Do none of you even care about Dantiel?" Baelac sends enchanted green leaflets down, revealing that the version of himself sitting at the table is a sham, a projection. Baelac is still broken and depressed, feeling more like a murderer than a brother let alone a hero. Ayton dissects the leaf and teleports away to sit beside Baelac.

"I know you're hurting, but it does none of us any good to sit idly by and let Kalypto ruin, well, everything."

"How can you move on so soon? Aren't you in mourning? He was our brother, and I murdered him brutally. I'm a monster, I'm a failure, and I let you down." He weeps.

"No, you didn't, Baelac. It wasn't you. It was Kalypto through you. It doesn't make you weak or evil or bad in any way. Don't you ever say that about yourself again. Do you hear me? You told me yourself you were struggling to fight against it. He's the most powerful monster in any world. There was nothing you could have done, and you heard our mother. She wants you to see it that way too. Believe me, there is a place for people who kill innocent lives intentionally, but that is not really for us to judge. We are not defined by mistakes. Everyone makes mistakes. What defines us is what we do with those mistakes. I know it hurts. I loved him too more than anything just like I love you, Baelac. You're all I have left of my family. I don't want anything to happen to you ever. But something did happen, and we must endure. We have to cope because the real threat behind it isn't you! It's never been you. Do you hear me? You're a good man. Without you, we would not have made it this far. You saved all of us. It was *not* you who killed Dantiel. Kalypto controlled you, and *he* did it. But that is beside the point. It has nothing to do with blame. The fact remains that because of a demon, our family is minus one. Do you think that slug of a beast is biding his time?"

"No, you're right."

"So what do we need to do?"

"We need to kill Kalypto and save our home." Baelac rises to his feet as he says that, wiping away his tears. Ayton smiles from behind.

Ayton and Baelac return downstairs where Isajella waits. Without a word, the three of them are all on the same page. Isajella grabs Ayton's hand and kisses it, thanking him for the talk he just had with Baelac. The Brothers Brea are absolutely determined. This will be the very last day of the existence of Kalypto, the Lord of Malice. Almost immediately and still without a single word, the two brothers run outside, and Baelac, with a green flash of his black pupil, hides and dismantles the fortress within the forest. Each foundational root and blossom slithers around the tree that supports them and withers away in a small puff of glitter, and it is as if there has never been a fortress in the first place.

"Do we know exactly where we're going? And what if the potion changed its nature just like the rest of the world?" asks Isajella, panting.

"I mean, those are good questions, but for now let's just worry about getting to it before Kalypto knows what we're doing, or the whole plan is off! We should split up that way he can't understand what were up to," suggests Baelac.

"Kalypto is not going to know a thing," Ayton says. Isajella and Baelac stop in their tracks and stare at him, both with a face asking him how.

"Happy birthday, brother." They all smile and cheer loudly, for on the anniversary of their birth, the villains have no power. So today, Kalypto will at most, summon his minions to do his work for him, and at best, Kalypto will take a sick day.

"You know it's amazing how that worked out. It's like…" he trails off as he realizes what he *finally* understood.

"It's like what, Baelac?" asks Ayton, hoping he knows the end of that sentence.

"It's like this is what we are supposed to do today. It's like fate." Baelac smiles. It feels empowering to feel like the very creator of the universe is cheering him on. It makes him feel he has a purpose and helps him focus on something other than the loss of Dantiel. He looks up at the sky, which is early sunrise, and he winks at the sun.

As the sun rises higher and higher, though, it is hidden almost immediately by the permanent black clouds covering all of the new Arkanya. The only light is from patches of black muck still burning from when the world died under the menace of Kalypto's Jigocrugya.

The three heroes run as hard as they can toward where they believe the potion of Nauz will be hidden. They reach the enchanted lake and admire it but continue running, enhanced magically by Baelac, giving them the speed of the wind at their feet.

On and on they run along the dead meadows and rolling hills of the blackened Arkanya. They think it strange that no monsters are disturbing them today and wonder if that is somehow a magical command by Kalypto for them to do. Either way, it is convenient for sure. Until suddenly, Ayton stops.

"HALT! We are not alone right now. Magic at the ready, brother," Ayton suggests. He is right, though. They hear the pitter-patter of some four-legged creature scurrying about ever closer to them.

Isajella has their backs and is prepared to fight with them, if necessary, as well. The creature approaches, and it is a small animal with the body from the waist down of a lion cub and the upper body of a weasel. He looks aged and tired.

"Who are you and why are you trespassing here?" asks Ayton.

"Trespassing? Oh no, great sir. I come but as a humble servant," says the weasel/lion, lowering his head.

"I'll not be asking again, or shall I kill you now and not risk my family?" asks Ayton.

"I come from a village in the northeast. My family was slain brutally by the gr…by the Lord of Malice himself." The animal begins to cry. "He used magic and trapped me upon a nearby tree and forced me to watch him eat my family and tear away their souls one by one. I can still hear their screams at night." He weeps. Isajella looks sad too. Ayton is extremely skeptical.

"We've all lost someone we love to that demon. Maybe you can help. We are—" Baelac is interrupted.

"Do not speak of our plans to a stranger!" Ayton hisses.

"What my friend means is that we have a very busy day, and while we offer our condolences, we really must be going" Ayton tries to wrap up this stressful conversation like a present.

"Leaving so soon? I mean don't you want to see my home?" urges the weasel.

"Oh no. Like I said, you may recall, we have not the time and must be going," Ayton emphasizes, slowly becoming agitated. Whatever the creature is doing, at the very least and most obviously, he is delaying them. But for what? Ayton speaks to his brother telepathically and warns him to say nothing more to the animal, ignore him, and keep running with Ayton. The animal follows suit.

"I can help! Tell me what you're doing, and I...maybe I can help you, please. You're all I have left in the world. I thought none but me survived. My life is without meaning, and I yearn for purpose again." The weasel weeps. What on earth is his deal? Is he acting, or is he legitimate? Is it worth the risk to find out? He remembers what his mother always says, "Be kind, have strength, and love always." So Ayton decides they will let him come.

Isajella votes no. Baelac and Ayton are unsure. "Does it matter what you think? He's following us!" cries Isajella. She is right. He is still following them close behind. They have to deal with the weasel.

Ayton figures it out. "He must be a servant of Kalypto. Think about what the guy is doing. He's delaying us. He's trying to make us waste our one day of Kalypto with no powers!"

And with that, the three quickly pivots and pins the weasel to the ground with their own magic.

"Here's the deal, weasel," Ayton begins.

"My name is..."

"Yeah, I know what your name is. Here's the deal. We know what you're playing at, and we're not going to let it happen. So you have two options. Option 1: We kill you right here, right now and carry on with our mission. Option 2: You go back to Kalypto and tell him we're coming for him. What'll it be?"

The weasel looks angry and confused.

"You seriously think I'd serve that hell demon? He's worse than all of Yamirzen curses combined. No. I hate him for the death of my family. I can never forgive him for what he did. You think after that trauma, that I would help him? You think I'm some weak weasel?" He is hurt. Or so it seems.

"You're, well, at least you half are," Isajella shakes her head. Now is absolutely not the time for jokes.

"I'll give you that, but there is not a damned thing he could do that would make me want to help him. I swear, if you tell me your plans, I can tell you his," replies the weasel.

"How can you tell me his plan if you don't help him?"

"I'm small. I fit in places no one notices, and I hear things. Calm down."

"GUYS, THIS IS AN ENORMOUS WASTE OF TIME. WE NEED TO KEEP MOVING," Baelac retorts. He takes matters into his own hands and magically traps the weasel in the tree beside him. Baelac is watching the sun as it now reaches near noon. Their only blessing of a day is almost half over.

"The only way you can escape this hold is by telling the truth, and I just want you to answer one question." Baelac is a genius. The weasel is terrified.

"What?" asks Will.

"What is your mission?"

There is a long stressful pause. Then the weasel takes a deep breath and answers.

"You've been right about me and wrong at the same time. My mission is to betray you and take you to Kalypto—" The weasel is not done, but Ayton is about to turn the weasel's blood to water and kill him.

"STOP! He's not finished. Let him speak first!" Baelac says.

"But I was truthful when I told you about my family, and I wanted to use this mission as a way to actually betray Kalypto instead. I understand if you don't believe me. I have no proof or evidence, and I have nothing left to lose. So actually, please just kill me so that I might reunite with my wife and my beautiful daughter." The half lion weeps. Isajella gets teary-eyed as well.

"When the fires began, I hurried my family into the cellar as I thought we'd be safer there, but the disgusting army was too quick, and they...they decapitated my daughter"—Will sobs—"right in front of me, my legacy was dashed in two. I screamed with terror, but that only attracted more of them, and they smiled at me through the smoke and fire and echoes of other families dying and killed my wife in the cellar. Kalypto picked me up and smiled and said, 'This is just the beginning.' I can't go on much longer, please let me die." The weasel weeps and weeps.

The magic holding him to the tree disarms, and the three heroes hold the lion tight and hug him.

"The Lord of Malice will be no more, I promise you. We are the Brothers Brea, the prophesied victors of Arkanya, and we come back to you now in the hopes that we can illuminate the darkness and bring an end to Kalypto's reign of poison," Ayton finishes.

"Before we tell you our plan, if you put one hair on the side of Kalypto, I will turn you into a puddle. Are we clear?" The weasel nods and thanks the heroes for their time and mercy.

"So how are you going to kill Kalypto? Are you going to give him happiness? asks Will. All of them stop dead in their tracks. Figuratively.

"What?" asks Baelac.

"Well, I thought you knew, do you not?" asks Will.

"Know what?" asks Ayton.

"Kalypto is the essence of hatred and is fed not by food or drink but instead by the happiness of others. He has no happiness of his own, so he steals it from anywhere he can find it. But that's the thing about happiness. If you steal it and kill to take it from someone else, it perverts into malice, greed, and revenge. Real happiness, joy, and peace are some things he has never had. So if you give it to him, he will break. He would shatter to oblivion. You are the prophesied heroes of Arkanya. You don't need any spells or weapons or magic items. It's in the great library, the one which Master Yidnar once presided over."

"You knew Yidnar? He was our creyfather," answers Ayton. Baelac smiles.

"That's incredible. He was my daughter's teacher and married my wife and I. Our family had the deepest respect for him. We saw what he did for you lot, and it made us, it made me hopeful that one day you'd return and bring light back to our home. You're the only ones who can," replies Will.

"Take us to Kalypto right now," says Ayton. Isajella is alarmed.

"What about the plan? What about getting him without magic and alone?" she asks worriedly.

"We have no need, if we get to him today. He already has no power. Take us to him."

"No! No, he'll kill you! He'll kill you!" Isajella weeps into his chest and feels Ayton's blue beating heart on her tearing eyes.

"Darling, you are the brightest light I could have ever hoped for. Just because I come from love doesn't mean I ever believed I'd be lucky enough to find it myself, particularly in the end times. I am whole with you. You've saved me in more ways than a person should be saved, but I love you, and nothing will ever take that away. You'll always be here, in my heart." He embraces his true love, and the sun pierces through the dark, black clouds for the first time since before the great fires of the Jigocrugya. Will is in shock.

He leads Baelac and Ayton to the fortress in the mountainside and says the Yamirzen magical words to open the gates. The gates are statues of slaves holding great structures above their heads made of black, stinking limestone, and they swivel around on an axis, letting them in.

"I hope you know what you're doing," replies Will.

"This is my destiny. If I die, then I'll be with my parents. If I survive, then I'll be with my brother and my true love. Either way, we win, the way I see it."

"Are you ready for a fight? It's probably going to be messy," Will clarifies.

"I was created for this. Let it be," Ayton says. He grabs his brother's hand and nods their heads in agreement. This is it; every moment of their lives has led them to this. Fate has aligned the days of the year perfectly to protect them, and their paths are true. But this is the end, and Kalypto stands just a yard away. He is weak they can tell, as this is a day he has no powers.

Will leaps to the foot of the dark throne and awakens the Lord of Malice.

"I brought them sire, the ones prophesied to ruin your darkness."

"I don't believe it. After all these years, we finally meet?" Kalypto stands and is the form of a huge, crowned skull with a twisting spine and two floating, massive claws but no fire and no smoke, just bones and armor.

"Let's finish this the way it truly began, wraith, just us," Ayton says.

Will leaps up high into the rafters, away from any collateral damage and watches on.

Kalypto laughs, and the castle trembles, crumbling chunks of stone from the ceiling down. His spell he cast the previous day is crafted in such a way that it activates a day later, so just a few moments ago, fire begins raining from the sky.

Isajella waits things out in the forest, but it soon catches ablaze. Kalypto laughs and smiles as he can only imagine that she is dead or dying.

Kalypto, Ayton, and Baelac dance in their duel around the fort, trying everything they can think of to bring forth Kalypto's own happiness, but nothing works.

Kalypto doesn't have magic, but he has slaves still and calls for his ancient Skrall Army to attack. He breaks an ebony Gothic vase and pours a thick bubbling muck from the tip onto the stone floor before him. First a worm-covered hand punches through, then another and another; a dozen climbs out of the tar-like mud and has magenta glowing crystals in their heads.

Baelac begins fighting them with his magic, conjuring vines to trap and strangle, creating the illusion of a forest to confuse them and let Ayton attack or encircling them with thorned bushes cutting them to pieces. For the moment, as Baelac's green magic flashes and sparks all over throughout the dark and fateful day, it seems as though they'll win. Then Ayton begins to put two and two together. These are not the original or normal Skrall Army he remembers. Those guys have swords for arms, and definitely nothing about them glows… He cuts off one's head and examines closer. As the seconds pass, the magenta crystal dims and dulls and turns to black. *That's it! They're just being powered by the crystals! Kalypto really can't do anything today can he?* He rejoices inwardly. He now digs out the crystal from this one Skrall's head and whispers to it, "When I put you in Kalypto's mind, show the happiness he cannot find." And it glows not green or black or magenta or even blue. Instead, it glows a brilliant, gleaming white.

Then he notices things are still and quiet. He looks up and sees that Kalypto has one last trick up his sleeve. He has pinned down Baelac to the ground and is using his thrice speak—a curse to induce suicide.

"No, Baelac, no! Don't look at his eyes! Look at me. Keep them on me!" But as Ayton approaches, Baelac has closed his eyes in the nick of time. He screams in agony as Kalypto begs to dig Baelac's eyes out, trying to force him to look at his eyes. Ayton secures the crystal and casts blasts and blasts of ice spears and falling chunks of frozen glaciers upon the demon. He then pierces Kalypto with an ice pear and shoves him off his brother whose face is covered in blood. Ayton isn't done ruining Kalypto's day. He has whispered something into his blue, glowing arms and casts a terrible spell of fierce power. An endless blast of boiling water streams into Kalypto's skull, and he forms an ice cage around him to trap him and tends to Baelac's wounds.

"No, no, Baelac, you're going to be okay! Stay with me!" Baelac looks behind Ayton and sees that Kalypto has shattered and exploded the ice cage and, slowly as if in slow motion, charges toward Ayton whose back is facing him. In this split-second moment, Baelac knows what he must do. He looks once more at his brother's eyes and smiles and says, "I'll always love you, brother. Let me do this." Baelac shoves Ayton away, and Kalypto therefore throws with all his weight his enormous claws deep into Baelac's chest. Ayton screams in protest as he watches his second brother die before him. He attacks the back of Kalypto with everything he has, out of anger, but it is no use. Nor does Kalypto care.

"Ayton, I had to, I gave you a chance. I need this. Let me die a hero, my sacrifice to redeem me from Dantiel." He sighs, and the green magic of his spirit fades and dims to no longer shining. Ayton screams once more, and as Kalypto is rejoicing with the death of another holy hero, Ayton stabs Kalypto right through his skull with the crystal of Pertez it turns out to be. Now enchanted by Ayton to inject one's lost happiness. Kalypto staggers and steps away from Baelac and collapses to the floor, sobbing. Ayton watches in confusion and is still weeping for his brother.

Kalypto roars and yells as flashbacks to his childhood comes rushing through, images of his mother putting his favorite flowers in his room while he was under the spell of his father, his mother combing his hair while he was sick in bed, images of when he was a boy before the days his father induced him into a magical coma, images of the only thing in any world that ever truly mattered—his family. Kalypto's skull cracks and crumbles, and the ground shakes in waves as pulse upon pulse of shock waves of energy shoots and explodes from the room, from Kalypto, and completely engulfs the entire land. Windows shatter, trees fall, Ayton screams with fear of the unknown, and more shock waves keep coming. Will jumps down from the rafters and is crying tears of joy, kissing Ayton's feet.

"You did it! You actually did it. This is it!" Will exclaims as the weasel part of his form withers away like dust and reveals that he is a true, magnificent, and strong lion with a golden-bronze fur coat and a rich, red mane. He jumps around the room, roaring with triumphant joy and happiness. He runs out to the balcony and urges Ayton to come watch. Ayton stumbles along the corridor and follows and collapses to his knees as he watches the incredible sight. The world is fixing itself. The darkest vile being has been undone, and with his vanquishing, Arkanya's magic is restored.

In Denebia, the enchanted forests blossom out of the dead ash and broken-in-half trees; they grow and soar ever upward into the sapphire skies. The Eirini River flushes away its toxic fumes and sparkles with its magnificent amethyst and sapphire waters of blessings and nourishment. In Regulusio, the mighty mines in the north mountains once again stand majestic and proud over Arkanya. In Leonulia, Yidnar's temple restores itself, and the angelic white marble becomes studded with emeralds and rubies in honor of Baelac and Dantiel respectively. Statues made of gold rose a hundred feet in their honor. The Palace of the Falls is also restored but this time at the same height as the rest of Arkanya, for no one is above anyone else. In Acamaro, the beautiful and food-enriched farmlands bloom like a rose opening in the morning dew and glisten with a thousand different crops and vegetables. Up high above all of them, Earth is also restored, descending with an impressive, controlled speed. The corner of the world that is magically extracted to save the heroes is returned to its rightful place and fill the meadows of the roses of deceit. In their absence, the Heatherlyn rose once again flourishes as far as the eyes can see, and at last, Arkanya is light and filled with peace. The survivors of Earth are reunited with their home world and are in tears and cheers of overwhelming joy that Ayton has succeeded. All that remains of Kalypto is his crown, which Ayton smashes in half and buries at the base of the Tree of Fayte.

Some of the former high-ranking members of government announce the following days that Arkanya, now saved, will begin restoration of life and will crown a new Rex and Rexa: Ayton and Isajella Brea. It is a glittering affair, and one that every soul loves and approves of more than anything. The Palace of the Falls as it once was called, will now be referred to as, The People's Palace and as such, will play host to visitors from other worlds, tourists from the Palace's nearby Palacorns, and the central governing headquarters. In homage to the fallen brothers, the south towers are white marble with inlaid rubies and emeralds. Likewise, the north towers represent the living hero, Ayton, and is with inlaid glimmering sapphires. All of the Earth dwellers are called upon the assemblage, and trumpets signal the Rex and Rexa of Arkanya, the High Archon Ayton Brea and his Rexa, Isajella.

"Though my brothers are sadly not here with us today, it is and always will be my solemn duty to protect, cherish, and love the people and world of Arkanya. For without the bravery of my fallen brothers, I would not be here to stand before you today. It was Dantiel who kept us all going when fear was overwhelming or when confusion stopped our plans or when we lost sight of who we are. It was he who taught me how to fight when you're scared because fear, though human, isn't helpful. No matter what we face, no matter how scary or dark or dismal, it doesn't last forever. You must hold onto hope, even if it's the smallest hope in the world. And it was Baelac who outsmarted every challenge we faced and taught me what it means to lead and to love, for no one showed those two things harder than he. There is no greater thing in life than love. In all its forms, love of a friend who encourages you when you're defeated, love of a wife who never leaves your side no matter the stakes, and love of family that will forever be with you even after death. So raise a glass, my friends. Like my brothers, be kind, have strength, and love always!" The world erupts in an eternal cheer and fireworks explode. Everyone is happier than the past hundred years, and Isajella kisses her Rex. Up in the clouds, the spirits of Baelac, Dantiel, and even Coragio and Puretia applaud and wink at Ayton from above. There is no doubt in anyone's mind that they, indeed, are the victors of Arkanya.

And they live happily ever after.

# About the Author

Anthony was inspired mostly by his own life for *The Victors of Arkanya*, his first published work. A lover of fantasy stories all his life, it wasn't until his penultimate year in college that a friend encouraged him instead of writing revisionist version of existing tales, to create his own. Fantasy stories, being Anthony's favorite, pave the way for a story to really come alive with a magic of its own. It is Anthony's wish that whoever reads this story is able to see through the symbols, find their meaning, and take valuable and helpful lessons he had learned in his own life in the past. The importance of happiness, the value of confidence, the gravitas and fragility of pain, and most importantly, discovering who you are as an individual are all themes he explored with this story. Every detail was explicitly chosen, every character particularly developed, every setting tediously described, all to set the stage for those and many more messages he hopes the reader can learn and enjoy.

CPSIA information can be obtained
at www.ICGtesting.com
Printed in the USA
BVHW021646200922
647510BV00019B/864